DEADFALL

OTHER BOOKS BY ANTHONY GIANGREGORIO

THE DEAD WATER SERIES

DEADWATER
DEADWATER: Expanded Edition
DEADRAIN
DEADCITY
DEADWAVE
DEAD HARVEST
DEAD UNION

ALSO BY THE AUTHOR

DEAD RECKONING: DAWNING OF THE DEAD
THE MONSTER UNDER THE BED
DEADEND: A ZOMBIE NOVEL
DEAD TALES: SHORT STORIES TO DIE FOR
DEAD MOURNING: A ZOMBIE HORROR STORY
ROAD KILL: A ZOMBIE TALE
DEADFREEZE
DEADRAGE
SOUL-EATER
THE DARK
RISE OF THE DEAD
DARK PLACES

DEADFALL

Anthony Giangregorio

DEADFALL

DEDICATION
This book is dedicated to my wife and best friend,
Jody

AUTHOR'S NOTE

This book was self-edited, and though I tried my absolute best to correct all grammar mistakes; there may be a few here and there. Please accept my sincerest apology for any errors you may find.

This is the second edition of this book.

Visit my website at undeadpress.com

Foreword

Greetings and welcome to my fourth book.

I still find it amusing to say that.

When I was in school I couldn't write a book report to save my life and even attempting to put pen to paper would have had me breaking out in hives.

So to have me writing twenty years after graduating high school is to say the least, ironic.

A close family member told me I impressed the hell out of them when they had found out I was writing. They said they couldn't believe I had it in me and that they were proud.

Despite the obvious compliment, you still can't help reading between the lines.

What they really meant to say was "Holy crap, I thought you were just another blue-collar shlub. I can't believe you were able to put all those words together into a real book!"

Now, I know what you're thinking. Anyone can throw a bunch of words together and say it's a book, but I'd like to think I write the way I would like to read someone else's work; with real characters that you care about in real situations and lots of action.

The characters need to be interesting and the plots need to at least seem to be real.

I don't know about you, but I can't stand reading a book or watching a movie where the creator decides to wave a magic wand for the sake of moving the story forward and completely destroys his or her own rules of believability.

Now, I won't deny some of my characters might be lucky, but any story of survival has 'lucky characters'. Whether it's because they find weapons to fight back or the keys to the car they need to escape in are in still the ignition.

After all, what defines luck over the simple will to survive and to do whatever is needed at all costs?

Besides, if the characters in the story weren't at least a little lucky, then wouldn't they be dead in the first chapter or five minutes into the movie.

What I'm trying to say is, I'm a realist, and with the exception of the dead walking, all the other rules and laws that make up the world we live in are still in place.

So while you read this book, say to yourself: "What would I do if I found myself in a similar situation? Would I hide in my cellar and wait to die when my food and water ran out? Or would I take he fight to the enemy and do whatever it took to survive. Whether that meant smashing my neighbor's head in with a shovel or shooting a stranger in the head when he attacked me, I'd do what had to be done.

While I may never be in the top ten bestsellers of the year, that's okay. If only a few people read my work and say: "Yeah, I liked it, it wasn't a bad read." Then I accomplished what I set out to do and will have hopefully left my mark on this small blue world we all live on.

And in the end, isn't that what we're all trying to do?

Anthony Giangregorio
January 2007

And their dead bodies shall lie in the streets of the great city…

Revelations
Chapter 11, Verse 8

And they of the people and nations shall see their dead bodies
and shall not suffer the dead bodies to be put in graves…

Revelations
Chapter 11, Verse 9

And if the plague be greenish or reddish in the garment, or in
the skin, or in anything of the skin; it is a plague…

Leviticus
Chapter 13, Verse 49

Prologue

In the vastness of deep space, a swarm of tiny meteors floated between the stars. Each one was no larger than a baseball, as they tumbled and drifted through the endless void of darkness.

Inside these small rocks was alien life, small worms really, that on a casual inspection might be considered nothing more than maggots.

They had lain dormant in their tiny prisons for thousands of years, the vacuum of space preventing them from reviving.

An infinite time later, time being meaningless in space, the meteors became caught in the gravity of a nearby planet.

Soon the meteors swirled down, heating up with the friction of reentry as they plummeted towards the blue planet below, the heat of reentry slowly reviving the dormant worms.

Down below, on the planet Earth, in the small, quaint town of Wakefield, Massachusetts, trick-or-treaters looked up as the small shooting stars streaked across the night sky.

"Make a wish, honey," one mother told her young son, upon seeing the lights in the sky. "They say its good luck," she finished.

The little boy closed his eyes and wished as hard as he could. He was about to tell his mom what he'd wished for when she put her finger up in a "no, no," gesture.

"No, honey, don't tell me your wish. If you do, it won't come true," his mother said.

The little boy nodded and smiled, then ran off to the next house on his route that night.

There were still a lot of houses to hit and a lot of room left in his candy sack.

The meteors continued through the layers of Earth's atmosphere, the metal in the spheres more than enough to prevent them from burning up on reentry.

The hundreds of meteorites split up from the turbulence and were sent flying across the United States to land in quiet towns and cities, more than half the east coast hit before the barrage was finished.

One lone meteor landed in an old, deserted cemetery behind an abandoned mortuary in Wakefield, Massachusetts, while others landed in the surrounding cities of Stoneham and Melrose.

The landing went unobserved, the small globe plowing into the ground, leaving a tear in the earth behind it.

Striking a heavy tombstone, the meteorite came to a stop, splitting open from the impact. The small worms within squirmed and fell to the leafy earth, the oxygen rich atmosphere causing them to suffer.

To escape the distasteful atmosphere, they dove into the soft mulch and began to dig deep to escape the air before it snuffed out their fragile lives.

Moving on instinct alone, they dug deeper into the soft ground, not knowing where they were going, but realizing they needed to escape if they were to survive.

Six feet under the ground, the worms came upon a carcass in a coffin; the wood surrounding the corpse shattered and rotted from age.

Immediately, they burrowed into the dead flesh, consuming it as they went.

A chemical by-product of their feeding was slowly saturating the desiccated cadaver.

This chemical slowly began to rebuild synapses and jumpstart the brain again inside the rotting corpse's body as the worms continued to feed and saturate the muscles and limbs.

Time went by quickly and in mere hours the dead hand of the corpse began to twitch. Minutes later, a rasping sound oozed from vocal cords that should never have spoken again and red eyes flared with awareness.

Suddenly, the corpse's arms shot up into the rotting top of its coffin. While dirt piled in, the now reanimated corpse crawled out; not knowing why, but knowing freedom from its prison was straight up.

Beside it in the other coffins, other corpses were slowly making their way to the surface of the earth, all filled with the, slimy squirming worms.

All of the corpses felt a hunger gnawing at where their souls once resided. They didn't know how to quench the feeling just yet, but would find out soon enough.

Chapter 1

It's Halloween night and all the friends and family of the Murphy's are gathered at their house for their annual Halloween bash. Inside the house, there are all sorts of monsters that only come out on Hallows eve. There's Bob from next door with his annual mummy costume. It looks old and worn, but that's only because he's worn it for five years straight.

There's Ruth from two houses over, wearing her French Maid uniform, maybe it would be a better costume if the whole neighborhood didn't know she wears it every weekend when she cheats on her husband with Bob, when her husband goes out of town.

Then Mary turns around and sees her husband. He's dressed up like a vampire and when he sees her in her skimpy jungle girl costume, he walks up to her and whispers something in her ear to the effect of: "Let's ditch our own party and go upstairs and make love."

She smiles and pushes him away, telling him: "We can't, we have guests."

Toby always gets frisky when she wears something skin tight.

Just then, the doorbell rings and Mary goes to the door. Out of habit she looks through the peephole to see who it is and her blood runs cold when she sees it's her mother-in-law.

The woman's cadaver-like face looks even more distorted through the peephole. Mary turns to her husband and mouths: "It's your mother."

He just smiles and tells her to let the woman in.

With a shudder that flows through her body, Mary pulls the throw rug that had bunched up to the door, so she can open it and welcome the only woman she hated most in the world.

Years ago, when she'd just been dating her husband, his mother had made clear her distaste for Mary and had done everything in her power to break them up. But like love often does, it prevails, and they had gotten married; and had two beautiful children; one already off to college in California.

Now, as she pulled the door open, she looked down at the old woman's shoes; hoping to delay the inevitable of looking at her for as long as possible. A pair of simple black Payless shoes stared back at her. Next was a pair of black stockings that covered the woman's skinny, varicose vein legs. Then her eyes took in her thin waist. When her breasts came into view, Mary could see one was missing.

Cancer had taken it many years ago and the woman showed the missing breast off like a trophy. In a way it was. She was a fighter. Mary wouldn't deny that.

Then Mary's eyes found her neck. The skin sagged a little like the beginnings of a rooster's wattle. But that's okay if you're eighty two.

Then, Mary's eyes finally rested on her face.

Actually, the face looked better in the peephole. The woman's face was pulled back as if haunted and there was a big honking wart on her chin. There was always one black hair sticking out of it and when she talked you would find yourself staring at it as it bobbed and weaved in the air with the movement of her jaw.

She looked like she was dressed like a witch and had left her wide, black hat at home, but when you looked closer, you'd see she was wearing black as her regular attire.

She was Italian you see, and when her husband had passed away a few years back, she had taken on the custom of only wearing black out of respect for him.

The funny part was when her husband was alive she drank constantly to dull the pain the bastard put on her and now acted like he was a saint.

Mary put on her best smile and welcomed the woman into her home. The old woman just shrugged and walked inside, acting as if Mary didn't even exist.

After years of this treatment, Mary just shrugged it off and would later beat the hell out of a pillow to let out all her pent up frustration.

The widow walked inside and was then lost amid the other revelers, soon finding her son. Toby hugged her and surely said the things sons are supposed to say to their mother's.

Mary checked her watch to see it was almost ten o' clock. Her daughter should be home soon. She hated it when she was out, but you had to let them leave the nest sooner or later and that's what she'd done. Still, Kim was her daughter and she loved her.

Her husband walked up to her and she pointed at her watch, the music making it hard to talk. He nodded and then put his mouth to her ear and told her their daughter had called and said she was at a friend's house and would be home by twelve.

Mary frowned. She didn't like her coming home so late, but if she was inside where it's safe, then what could be the harm?

Putting it out of her mind, she turned and rejoined her guests, with her husband by her side.

It was a long time until this party would wind down and she had a lot of work to do to keep it going.

*   *   *

Kim closed her cell phone and turned to her boyfriend, Joey.

"All set, they think I'm at a friend's house," she said while walking around the room.

Her other friends were there, too, Paul and Linda, who were talking softly together in a corner of the room.

They had all decided instead of doing the traditional crap for Halloween, they'd sneak into the abandoned mortuary by the cemetery to really get the feel of Halloween.

So after they'd fooled all their parents into thinking they were at each other's houses, they went to the mortuary where they'd have a little make-out session and drink some of the beer Joey had pinched from his dad's cellar earlier that day.

They stood in front of a window that overlooked the street. The street was deserted mostly because the mortuary was situated on an abandoned cul-de-sac.

Outside, the wind blew what was left of the fall leaves onto the black, barren street, where they would then blow away with a sound like crinkling paper.

A half-moon bathed the street in an eerie glow that cast shadows wherever the light was blocked.

All in all a pretty creepy street, straight out of your average horror movie.

Paul was pretty handy with electronics and so had jury rigged a small camera to the front of the building, so if anyone came by, they'd know.

In the flickering light of the small monitor, his face gave off a ghostly pallor that only increased when he would look away from the screen.

"All clear, there's no one around," he said.

Kim nodded while Joey walked up behind her and put his arms around her. She smiled at his warmth and cuddled up against him.

"Hey, have you guys heard about the stories they say about this place?" Joey asked with an evil smile.

"What stories?" Paul asked, knowing where the conversation was going and not wanting it to. But once Joey got started, that was it.

"What stories? How about the one about the caretaker who had a heart attack and was found dead two years after he died, but yet every Halloween people would see him in the window as he continues to watch over his charge," Joey said in the spookiest voice he could manage. "You know, his body is buried out back in the cemetery," he finished

Kim pushed back against him and gently elbowed him in the ribs. "You're so full of it, you know that? Come on, let's have a beer."

Joey smile. "Okay, but I tell you this land is haunted and don't be surprised if we see him later. They say his skin is all dry and his chest is ripped open from the autopsy."

"Stop it, Joey, I mean it. If you don't stop trying to scare me I'm leaving," Kim said.

"All right, relax, I'm sorry," Joey said, pausing to crack open a beer.

For the next hour the friends sat around swapping stories and drinking, the wind howling in the street outside the dirty windows of the mortuary.

*   *   *

Deep inside the cemetery, more dirt began to shift, as other undead creatures were revived.

Slowly a hand pushed through, maggots falling from where they were dislodged from in between rotting fingers.

Slowly an arm came into view, the cadaver pulling itself free of its tomb.

Then another hand pushed through, sending clumps of dirt everywhere. With two desiccated arms now free, the head of what was once a man started to push free of the ground, like a sick parody of birth with red eyes flashing in the darkness.

One eye was missing, and as the head cleared the ground, earth worms squirmed in the empty eye sockets, angry their meal was moving.

The face resembled a rotten potato more than anything human; pieces of flesh falling to the ground around it. Within another moment it had pulled itself free up to the waist and the remnants of a black suit could clearly be seen in the half-moonlight.

Then the creature lost its balance and fell to the ground with a thud, barely discernable on the sod of leaves.

Now crawling, the ghoul dragged itself along the ground, pulling its feet out of the hole.

With a sucking sound, one of its shoes stayed behind as the reanimated corpse brought itself to a standing position.

Legs that weren't meant for standing ever again now supported the cadaver as it took its first hesitant step forward.

The shoeless foot came down in the soft leaves and a second later the other foot followed. Motion became a little easier as long unused limbs began to loosen.

Behind it, more graves were disgorging its contents, and when they had also risen from the cold ground, the swarm of walking dead began stumbling towards the mortuary, following the others that had risen before them.

In the surrounding darkness, only the glow of their red eyes showed they were there.

They had unfinished business, and no matter what happened this night, that business would be concluded before the moon left the night sky.

Chapter 2

John Monroe veered off of Interstate 95, taking the off ramp to North Avenue in Wakefield.

The short commute to work from his tiny one bedroom apartment in Stoneham was nice and quick, just the way he liked it.

He never understood why someone would work an hour away from where they called home. All those hours wasted on the road everyday as they drove to and from work.

Nope, quick and easy, that's the way Johnny liked it, or at least that's what his mother used to call him.

He hadn't been called Johnny in a few years, since his mother passed away. Heart failure, she'd only been sixty-five years old.

Now he was alone with all his family dead.

He'd been married for about five years, finally tying the knot when he'd turned thirty.

His wife, Julie had been ten years younger than him and they had been in love.

Just last year they had bought a house together, the first one for him and her.

For the next six months they'd been happy, enjoying their new home and making plans to start a family.

Then she'd gotten a part time job at one of the local pubs in the area and had discovered a night life that the two of them had never really explored together.

Almost overnight, Julie became unhappy, always arguing with him to go out and party, but after working all day, he was tired and just wanted to relax in the new home he had worked so damn hard to finally get.

Then one day a few months later, totally out of the blue, Julie said she wanted a divorce, that she wasn't happy anymore, that she wanted more for herself then just lying around watching television every night.

He had been floored, never seeing it coming. He'd always taken good care of her, giving her whatever she'd wanted and then some. Now, when they had finally achieved the American dream of owning their own house, she wanted to pull the rug out from under him.

He had agreed to the divorce, not wanting to be with someone that didn't love him and had later found out that she'd been cheating on him behind his back.

That was what really pissed him off. He'd found out later, they had even done it in his own bed when he was at work.

After finding out about the betrayal, the gloves had been off.

The divorce lawyers had handled their finances and the first thing to go was the house.

It nearly ripped his heart apart to have to sell the one thing he'd worked so hard in his life to finally attain. But he didn't have a choice. The mortgage was too high for him to swing on his own, so the house had been sold and the money split between the two of them.

With all the stress of the divorce, he'd faltered at work and had lost his job. He couldn't really blame them for firing him.

Now, he worked security for a small operation out of Malden. The pay wasn't great, but it more than covered the rent for his small apartment.

He frowned for a moment as another car drove by him with their high beams on.

Turning down a side street he drove down Main Street. Checking his watch, he was pleased to see he still had fifteen more minutes until he would have to relieve Tod at work.

John noticed something going on up the street and slowed his small Honda Civic down, finally coming to a stop in front of a few saw horses. The road was blocked off. It looked like the town was having a small block party.

Then he remembered the article in the newspaper.

It was Halloween night after all and the town had thrown a block party for all the kids.

Sitting in his car watching the revelers, he felt a small tinge of jealousy. That should be him in there with all those other families, his nonexistent child on his shoulders while they played games together.

The car behind him beeped politely, shaking him from his stupor.

Driving on, he followed the detour the young cop was pointing to.

When John was side by side with the young policeman he noticed the guy looked like he had just graduated from high school, the face looking like he was barely old enough to shave.

The policeman nodded politely at John as he drove by and a second later was behind him as the flow of traffic continued up the detour.

John followed the street, not totally aware of where he was. He had only had the security job for a few weeks and had only known the one way to get to work.

Sighing heavily, he looked at his watch. Tod was going to kill him for being late, but there was nothing he could do about it.

He stopped at a stop sign, not quite knowing which way to go. A group of children walked by the front of his car, with parents following discreetly behind them.

A mother looked at him through the windshield and smiled as she passed. John returned the smile with one of his own and decided to take a right.

He followed the street for another mile until he decided he was lost.

He was turning around in a small cul-de-sac when all of a sudden something jumped out at the front of his car!

The shadowy figure bounced off the front bumper and then rolled in the street, stopping a few feet in front of his car.

John stopped the car with a screeching of brakes and jumped out, his mind already trying to figure out how to deny what had just happened.

It wasn't his fault. Whatever he'd hit had appeared out of nowhere.

Slowly he walked to the shrouded figure, trying to put off what he'd find for as long as possible.

His right hand had his cell phone in it as he crept up to what he was sure was a body, his fingers already dialing 911.

A second later, he heard an operator's voice coming from the tiny speaker in his phone.

"911, what is the nature of your emergency?" The robotic voice asked.

"Uh, yeah, hi. My name is John Monroe and I think I just hit a guy with my car," John said, shakily.

"All right then, sir. What is your location?" The robotic voice asked.

"Ah. I'm not quite sure. I got lost and then the guy, umm, wait a sec, let me check for a street sign," John said, while he began searching for the green sign.

A moment later in the shadows from the overhanging trees he saw a small green sign on the standard black pole proclaiming he was on Linden Street.

"Ah, okay, I'm on Linden Street. So what do I do now?" He asked.

"Just stay calm and wait for the paramedics. A police unit has been dispatched, as well."

"Oh, okay, thanks, I guess," John said, a little uneasy as what had happened began to sink in. He might have killed a guy. Would he be found at fault, would he go to jail for vehicular homicide?

Before he could put his cell phone away it rang again and he absently answered it. "Hello?"

"Hey, John, it's Tod. Where the hell are you? You should have relieved me ten minutes ago," Tod said, clearly pissed off.

"Oh, shit, sorry, man, but I just got into some trouble and I don't know when I'll be there," John said in a daze.

Tod started spouting some crap about how he better get his ass to work when John shut the phone off. He had enough problems right now without listening to Tod bitch about staying late.

He stood in the middle of the deserted street looking down at the body he'd just hit. The stench coming off it was overwhelming, so he turned his face away to breathe some fresh air.

Had he hit a bum, maybe?

A few minutes later, he heard sirens, the ambulance finally arriving.

John studied at his watch and was impressed. Less than eight minutes had passed since he had called 911. The ambulance pulled up to him, lights flashing, bathing everything in a red and yellow glow.

The two paramedics jumped out of their vehicle, quickly moving to the back to retrieve what they needed to hopefully save the bum's life.

While this was happening, a police squad car pulled up as well, blue lights adding to the other colors illuminating the area.

John stood where he was, waiting for the cop to exit his car and walk over to him.

He was mildly amused to see it was the same young cop he'd seen at the detour.

The kid hitched up his pants, which were obviously weighted down by his gun belt, and walked over to him with a stride that almost made John snicker.

The kid already had his notebook out, his eyes taking in the scene in front of him.

Meanwhile, the paramedics had retrieved their medical supplies and were now running to the body.

"What happened here?" The young cop asked in a wise ass voice that immediately put John on edge. The question was so redundant John couldn't help but be a wiseass, too.

"My date and I had a fight, so I ran him down with my car," he quipped.

The cop frowned, about to say something back when one of the paramedics yelled out.

"Hey, what the hell's going on here? Is this some sort of a Halloween prank?" The paramedic called out to John.

"Prank, what are you talking about?" John asked, while he and the cop walked over to the paramedics.

"Look at this guy. He sure as hell isn't alive. This guy's been dead for years. Hell, the smell alone is a dead give away."

John and the cop walked over to the others, looking down on what was obviously a corpse.

"Jesus, guys, I don't know what to tell you. I swear I ran this guy down," John said.

The other paramedic was busy packing up his gear when the corpse's eyes snapped open, red eyes glowing malevolently.

The paramedic still hadn't noticed anything unusual, while his partner stood up to talk with John and the cop after he'd finished packing his own gear.

Leaning one hand against the street for leverage, he started to stand up.

Before his hand left the street the corpse rolled over and sank its rotting teeth into the paramedic's arm.

The man screamed in shock and pain, trying to pull his arm away, but the teeth had sunk in too deep.

With another panicked heave, the paramedic yanked his arm out of the bloody mouth, blood spraying everywhere.

John just stood there, his jaw hanging down. What he was a witness to was utterly impossible.

The corpse didn't even have any organs, the autopsy scar clearly visible under the torn and tattered shirt.

The visceral scene was too much for the young policeman and he turned away and threw up his dinner all over the street.

Meanwhile, the paramedic was scrambling away from the now fully active corpse, the rotting, desiccated body pulling itself along the street after the hapless man.

Panic erupted, while the other paramedic ran to his partner, trying to staunch the flow of blood; his partner's shrieks of pain echoing off the other buildings.

The cop had come to his senses and John grabbed him by the arm.

"Well, don't just stand there. You're a cop for Christ's sake. Help them!" John screamed at the young man.

The cop seamed to snap out of whatever stupor he was in and then looked at John.

"You stay here," he ordered John.

John nodded, not having a problem with the order in any way.

The cop moved closer to the crawling corpse, still not quite comprehending what was happening. He leaned down and grabbed the corpse by its feet, dragging it back to John's Honda. The corpse flailed its arms wide, trying to find purchase on the pavement, but finding none.

When the cop had pulled the flailing body far away from the paramedics, he looked at John.

"What the hell do I do now?" He squeaked. Then he had to jump back when the creature sat up and tried to take a bite out of him.

John just shrugged. "Sorry, man, I don't have too much experience with dead people who walk around. Come on, this can't be real. It has to be some kind of Halloween prank, or something."

"I'd like to agree with you, but trust me; this isn't a guy in a costume," the cop said.

John's eye caught movement from the edge of his vision. Squinting into the darkness at the edge of the flashing lights, he thought he saw other figures moving around.

John took a closer look at his surroundings, realizing he'd had his accident in front of a mortuary.

On the front of the building's walkway was an old sign that read: **MANCHESTER MORTUARY**, in bold letters.

Below these faded and peeling words was another sign that read: **MANCHESTER CEMETERY.**

"Nice," John mumbled. Of all the places to be on Halloween night, he found himself at a mortuary with a live, dead corpse walking around.

John looked over at the paramedics. They seemed to be doing okay.

He couldn't help it, his curiosity getting the better of him, so he walked over to the two men. He had to jump away from the corpse when it tried to grab him.

"Nice try, pal, but the jig is up, why don't you give it a rest," he said.

The man that had been bitten was covered in sweat, his friend having just given him a shot of morphine for the pain.

The bandage was soaked in blood and the unhurt paramedic was changing the dressing for the second time.

In the headlights of their van John saw the open wound for a split second before a new bandage was applied.

John would have sworn later that he's seen maggots squirming around in the blood of the open wound. But that would be impossible, the man had just been bit by what obviously was a Halloween prank gone bad, and there was no way the wound could be infected so quickly.

He was about to comment on this fact to the other paramedic when those shadowy figures he'd seen a few minutes before came into clarity.

There was a group of people, at least ten or twelve, from John's quick count, who were wearing the best zombie costumes he'd ever seen.

They shambled out of the darkness and with moans and groans stumbled into the street, their eyes glowing in the feeble light.

"Wow, this is great. It's like something out of a Romero movie," John said, fascinated by the scene in front of him.

He watched with amusement as five of the people surrounded the two paramedics. John's face went from amusement to shock when the walking corpses sank their teeth into the two trapped men.

Their screams for help quickly turned to shrieks of pain, skeletal hands dug into soft flesh, ripping and pulling until the street was running red with the dying men's blood.

John couldn't believe what he was watching. Had a mental insane asylum let loose all of its deranged prisoners, who were now on a killing spree in the suburbs of Wakefield, Massachusetts?

John stood absolutely still, too scared to move when the young cop's voice drifted over to him. The kid was at his squad car with his radio sticking out of the window. The kid had grabbed it and was even now calling in for more backup.

Then the kid ran up to John and pulled him by the arm. "Look, mister, whatever's going on here, you don't need to be here, so get goin'."

"Shit, officer, you don't have to tell me twice," John said, rushing back to his car.

Climbing in, he slammed the car in drive and after a few attempts at backing up; he was able to get out from between the squad car and the ambulance.

He floored the gas pedal and shot back down the street, taking a quick look in his mirror.

The flashing lights made it hard to pinpoint any one thing out of the darkness, but he definitely saw the cop pull his weapon from his hip, and just before John turned a corner and was long gone, he distinctly heard the sound of gunshots.

Then he was back on the main road, and with a few rights and lefts, he found himself only a few minutes from work. Shook up and moving on autopilot, he drove to work to relieve Tod. Not really knowing what else to do.

Chapter 3

Inside the mortuary, the four friends were still hanging out. Paul had a pretty good buzz on and Joey and Kim had snuck away for a little make out session.

Paul wandered over to the monitor to check if things were cool outside. He hadn't checked for more then an hour and was surprised to see the street in front of the mortuary was a hive of activity.

Flashing lights from an ambulance and a police car shone across the street, bathing everything in a warm glow.

"Oh, shit, cops," he said, his buzz partially gone now.

He decided he better tell the others. It was time to go. If he got caught in the mortuary, trespassing and drinking, he didn't even want to know what his dad would do to him.

Something painful, definitely.

Linda was in another room playing solitaire. They'd had a disagreement a few minutes ago about when she was going to put out for him.

The discussion had ended with him being told to: "Fuck off and go play with himself," so he'd decided to go check the monitor.

And was he glad he did.

Moving through the dark hallways of the mortuary, he was soon walking through the doors to Linda's room in less than a minute.

She looked up when he walked in and snarled at him.

"I didn't change my mind, so you can just forget about trying to talk me into it," Linda said.

Paul waved his hands in front of him. "Relax, Linda, that's not why I'm here. We got cops out front. We've got to go, now. I can't get caught here, my dad'll kill me."

Suddenly, gunshots sounded out front.

Paul ducked instinctively.

"Oh, shit, what the hell was that, gunshots?" He asked, clearly scared.

"If it was, then you're right. We need to go, now. Come on, let's get Joey and Kim and get the fuck out of here," Linda told him, throwing the cards to the floor, her game forgotten.

"Okay, that's what I'm talking about," Paul said, moving for the door with Linda behind him.

By the time they reached Kim and Joey's room down the hall the young couple was already on their feet.

At the moment they were busy fixing disheveled clothes that had been undone in their bout of heavy petting.

When Paul and Linda plowed through the partially open door, they looked at their two friends.

"We got cops outside. We need to get the hell out of here, now!" Paul exclaimed while going to the window to try to see the street. The room was on the far side of the building and all he could see were trees that needed a good trimming.

"Did you hear that loud sound? That wasn't what I think it was, was it? I mean, all we heard were a few cars backfiring. That's what it was, right?" Joey asked, finishing with his shirt buttons.

Shaking his head Paul looked at his two friends.

"Sorry to be the one to break the bad news, but I've gone hunting with my dad and I know the difference between a car backfiring and a gunshot. And that was a gunshot," Paul said.

"That's crazy; this is Wakefield, not Lowell. Why the hell would there be a gunfight outside an abandoned mortuary?" Kim asked, perplexed.

"Look, why the fuck does it matter. Let's go. There are cops outside and I'm supposed to be at your house, remember?" Linda said to Kim. "If I get caught lying to my folks again, then I'll end up being grounded until Christmas. So can we please go?"

"Sure, Linda, we can go. It's getting late anyway. Besides, I told my dad I'd be home by twelve."

Paul and Linda smiled. "Good, then let's go. I'll come back tomorrow and get my monitor and other equipment. I'm sure it's safe here, anyway."

With the four friends agreeing on leaving, they started to gather what they'd brought with them and in another five minutes were ready to go.

Moving through the dark halls with nothing but the wan light coming in through the few dirty windows, the four friends headed for the door to the outside.

The closer they got to the door, the more noise they began to hear.

More gunfire was mixed with screaming and yelling. The screams making all four of them begin to cringe in terror.

"What the fuck is going on out there that would make cops yell like that?" Joey whispered.

"Whatever it is, I don't think I wanna find out anytime soon," Paul answered back.

"You two shut up, you're not helping," Kim snapped. She was scared, too, but talking about it wasn't helping.

They moved the few remaining feet to the outside door and stopped as one entity.

Joey was the first in line and after Paul gave him a nudge, he reached for the doorknob.

With his heart in his throat, he slowly opened the door.

The chaos outside flooded into the small hallway; the reality of what was happening beyond the door sinking in.

Although they were all too young to remember WW2 they had all seen movies and that's what they thought of as they looked out onto the once deserted street.

Since Paul had looked at the monitor, ten more minutes had passed, and there were now three police cars, plus the ambulance in the small cul-de-sac.

The street was littered with bodies. In their few short years on earth the four teenagers had lived a life of luxury, never wanting for anything, nor suffering.

What they now saw in front of them couldn't compare to anything from their own sheltered lives. Only what they'd seen in the movies could compare.

And all four of them would agree if they were asked. That the real thing is nothing compared to what someone might see on television or the movies.

The first thing they noticed was the smell, like copper. They didn't realize it, but they smelled the gallons of blood that was now covering the street from all the dead men and women.

Other people were leaning over the bodies, probably trying to help the wounded, Kim thought, peeking around her friends to see outside.

"What are we waiting for, let's go," Linda said from the back of the line.

"Hold on, I just want to make sure it's safe. You don't want to get caught, do you?" Joey asked.

Linda just mumbled something under her breath.

Joey shook his head, God she was such a bitch. He didn't have any idea what Paul saw in her.

Psyching himself a little more, Joey opened the door and stepped outside, the others on his heels.

The people in the street didn't seem to notice them and that was fine with Joey. Moving as quietly as he could, he sneaked away from the door, hugging the walls of the building to hopefully stay in the shadows; the others right behind him.

When Kim exited the building she paused for a second, looking out into the street at the carnage.

She spotted a man leaning over a police officer, giving the wounded man CPR. The man kept leaning forward to give the policeman air and would then lean back to take a breath.

Kim watched, mildly curious for a few moments. Then the man leaned in one more time and gave the man air. When he pulled his head back, he turned to look in Kim's direction, his eyes seeming to glow red; or was that a trick of the strobe lights?

Kim stared in horror at the bloody countenance. The lights from the emergency flashers hit the man's face; in his mouth there was a piece of meat that looked an awful lot like a tongue.

The policeman's tongue? But if that was true, then that would mean...

The eyes of the killer spotted her and her friends and the ghoulish mouth spread into a smile, the tongue flapping back and forth like a half dead fish.

Kim stared at that face for another second and then let out a scream that floated across the street. She didn't want to, but it just came out of her throat on its own volition.

All the people who had been helping the wounded men in the street stopped what they were doing and looked up. Heads turned to the sound of the scream and in half a second every bloody face was looking in the direction of the four friends. That was when Kim realized those people were not helping the wounded.

"Oh, shit, what the fuck did you do that for?" Joey asked from her side.

"Oh my God," she said, pointing at the man with a tongue in his mouth.

"I think that man is eating that other man," she finished.

"What? That's ridiculous, come on, let's get going before the cops stop us," Paul said while moving along the building.

The others followed and in another minute they were in the parking lot behind the mortuary and ready to get into Kim's car.

With a sigh of relief, everyone waited for Kim to find her keys so they could leave.

*   *   *

Out front on the now bloody street, the policemen's bodies lay silent, while the undead feasted on them.

While the ghouls ate, the parasitic worms were transferred to the new host bodies. The worms immediately started to eat, leaving their chemical behind in their wake.

When a sufficient amount of the fluid was in the now dead policemen and paramedics, their lifeless bodies began to twitch.

Upon the first sign of movement, the ghouls stepped away from their meal, no longer interested in the dead flesh.

The craving they felt was for only live meat.

Slowly, eyes snapped open and limbs started moving, only now hampered by missing tendons and muscle.

One of the paramedics had his whole torso ripped open, his organs pulled out while the walking corpses had fed. Now the man raised himself onto unsteady legs, the rest of his loose organs spilling onto his shoes and the pavement.

On wobbly legs, the newly revived zombie stumbled across the street and to the sidewalk. Inside his chest, hundreds of the parasites squirmed and fed.

One by one the slaughtered police officers climbed back to their feet, slowly walking towards the mortuary.

The more they walked, the more adept they became, and soon they were moving at a brisk clip, one part fast walk, one part jogging. The other ghouls, having been dead for years could only shamble slowly, their muscle mass not up to any form of fast locomotion. Within a minute they were moving around the side of the mortuary, walking straight for the parking lot.

In the lead of the undead group was the first ghoul to spot the four friends. The tongue from the slaughtered policeman was now devoured and the cold, dead eyes watched the young meat only moments away.

Spotting the fleeing humans in the shadows of the moonlight, the ghoul picked up its pace, its blood-red mouth already tasting the sweet flesh.

*   *   *

Kim continued to dig around in her purse, but couldn't seem to find her keys.

"Shit, Kim, come on. We've got to go before they see us back here," Joey said from her side.

"I know, what the hell do you think I'm doing? I know they're in here, just give me another second."

Sounds of moaning and the scuffing of feet on the dry leaves on the lawn made the group look up.

Paul stared in horror, seeing at least ten people coming over the lawn straight at them. In the reflection of the streetlights, he could clearly see badges on some of the chests of the men moving towards them.

"Shit, Kim, I think our luck just ran out, look," Paul said, pointing to the cops approaching them.

Kim looked up from her search for her keys, thinking she was so dead when her parents found out about this, when she got a better look at the first people in line.

Their faces were covered in blood, the front of their clothes a dark vermilion color.

But it was when they moved a little closer that she knew something was off about these people. It was their eyes, they seemed to glow red. Even from where she was, still a fair distance away, she saw it.

Immediately she started digging in her pocket book again, realizing it was their only way out of the mess they were in.

"I'll go stall them; you guys get in the car, but don't leave without me," Joey said, moving back up the slight incline of the lawn to cut off the police before they got to them.

Kim looked up; her attention focused on her keys and didn't hear what Joey had said. By the time she realized what he'd done it was too late to stop him.

She watched in horror as Joey stopped in front of the group of people and she saw his hands moving in the air.

When Joey talked, his hands were always in motion; that was just his way, she had always found it endearing.

Paul let out a sigh of relief when Joey started talking to the police.

"Hey, look, I think it's gonna be all right, I think he's doing it," Paul said from the other side of the car.

But then it all went terribly wrong.

One second Joey was standing there, his arms flying around him, while he told the police a crazy story of why they were at the mortuary on Halloween night.

And the next second he was being overwhelmed by bodies, dragging him to the soft loom, where they proceeded to rip him apart.

When his first bout of screams floated to the others at the car, Paul took off at a run, going to help his friend.

Half a minute later, he was kneeling down on the ground, pushing the awakened corpses away from him. It only took a matter of a heartbeat for Paul to realize what he'd done when he chose to run to his friend's aid.

He fell back onto his butt and tried to crawl away backwards, but didn't get three feet before the other bodies swarmed over him, ripping and biting at his flesh.

Linda stared in horror and then let out a blood curdling scream of her own while she watched her boyfriend being torn apart, limb by limb.

Paul wouldn't be coming back from the grave. The ghouls weren't planning on leaving enough leftover for that to happen.

Kim's hand grasped her lucky keychain and with a triumphant waving of the keys in the air she stuck them in the lock of the driver's door and pulled it open.

On the other side of the car, Linda stared in shock, not believing what she'd just witnessed.

"Linda, get in the damn car!" Kim yelled.

But Linda didn't hear her and just continued staring at the visceral scene only twenty feet in front of her.

Kim started the engine on her little Toyota and put the car in reverse.

Lowering the passenger side window, she yelled at Linda one more time.

"Linda, will you get the fuck in the damn car!"

Linda snapped out of her shock for a moment and turned to stare at Kim, her eyes not really seeing her.

"Get in the car, you goddamn idiot, before they get you, too!" Kim yelled again, revving the engine to make her point.

To Kim it seemed an infinite slowness, but Linda finally opened the passenger door and sat down. Kim floored the car and backed out of the parking lot, the zombies only seconds behind her.

With the car pointed in the right direction, she floored it, the first corpses in line rubbing their hands against the cool metal of her car while she shot out of the driveway and headed for the street.

The street was blocked by all the cruisers, so she pointed the nose of the car for the sidewalk.

Jumping the curb, she struggled to maintain control of the little car and in another moment was free of the cul-de-sac and was heading down the street way too fast.

Reaching the end of the street, she almost hit a late night trick or treater.

While she swerved to avoid him, she noted he was a teenager, obviously up to no good, as it was well after midnight.

Her car plowed into the fire hydrant at the end of the street, the car rising into the air before the undercarriage caught on the hydrant, knocking it flat to the sidewalk.

The sound of snapping metal floated up to her while she was being jostled around inside the car, and when it was over, she opened her door and fell out to the street. She had a small cut on her forehead from her head striking the windshield, but other than that she was fine.

Climbing to her feet, she looked into the car to see how Linda was. Her friend's eyes were open, but she wouldn't be seeing anything ever again. Her neck was at an unnatural angle and a small ribbon of blood dripped from her mouth.

"Oh my God," Kim said to the air. "I killed my best friend."

She ran around to the passenger side and opened the door. The second the door swung open, Linda's lifeless body fell out.

Kim was there to catch her and she gently laid her down to the soft grass on the sidewalk.

Reaching for a pulse, she prayed to find one, but after a full two minutes realized it was hopeless. Her friend was gone.

Moaning drifted to her from down the street she had just vacated.

In the gloom of the night, she could see tiny red lights bobbing in the air, about five to six feet off the ground.

She knew she only had minutes to decide what to do. She didn't want to leave her friend, but what else could she do?

Pulling her purse from the car, she grabbed her cell phone and dialed 911.

After two rings she heard a tape recorded message.

"We're sorry, due to overwhelming calls we are unable to answer your call at this time, please stay on the line and we will be with you as soon as possible." Then the message began to repeat itself.

Kim stared at the phone with a creased brow, like she could will someone to answer her with the power of her mind. Then decided it was hopeless and pressed the end button on her cell phone.

With the ghouls only a minute away, she shoved her phone back into her purse and decided she would have to get home on foot.

She turned and with one last look at her friend and tears in her eyes, took off at a run, leaving the ghouls behind.

Her house was only a mile and a half away and she was in good shape.

She figured if there were no more problems tonight, she should be home in about half an hour. She'd explain about her friends and the car to her parents tomorrow. For now she just wanted to climb into her bed and cry.

With the sounds of more chaos drifting to her from other streets, she ran for all she was worth.

Chapter 4

Mary stood in the corner of her house, watching her guests enjoying themselves.

She loved being a host to the parties she would throw. Every Halloween and Christmas the whole block would show up.

As soon as this party was over, she'd already be planning the Christmas one.

To put on a good party took a lot of work, good planning and a little bit of luck. Her own mother had taught her that and it had been true for every party she'd ever thrown.

Her husband was in the corner with his mother, talking about God knew what.

Mary tried to pretend she wasn't watching, but she couldn't help herself. Her mind kept wondering what that evil woman was placing in her son's head.

Through the din of the music and people talking, Mary heard the doorbell ring.

Forgetting her family problems for the moment, she went to the door to see who it could be. It was well after midnight and as far as she knew everyone who wanted to come was already here.

Looking through the peephole in the door she was surprised to see four men in what looked like zombie costumes.

Opening the door with a smile, she stepped back to welcome them inside.

"Wow, your costumes are great, who's under all that makeup?" She asked, but then decided it didn't matter. The fun of Halloween is that sometimes you don't know who is under the mask.

"Come on in, there's plenty to eat. I'm sure you'll get your fill," Mary finished waving them inside.

For a moment they just stood there, swaying gently back and forth. Mary noticed they all had red eyes. She thought how neat it was and figured they must use contact lenses for the desired effect.

Finally, as if deciding he wanted to come in, the first man in line walked into the house, followed by the other three.

Outside in the street, the sound of screaming came to her ears, loud enough to be heard over the party goers inside her house.

She smiled to herself. Obviously someone else was having a wild time on Halloween night. After all, this was the night to be bad.

When the last man had walked by, her she had to hold her nose.

Wow, what a smell. They smelled like they'd come from the grave itself. Talk about authenticity.

The four men were soon lost in the crowd, the party kicking into high gear before everyone called it a night.

The police in Wakefield usually gave her a break until at least one in the morning. After that, she knew to keep the noise down or risk receiving a visit from the boys in blue.

From somewhere across the house she heard someone shriek.

Screaming with pleasure she assumed. Moving back to the party, she decided to go to the kitchen and see how they were set for alcohol.

Walking into the kitchen, she saw one of the late arrivals in a zombie costume in the corner of the room with her neighbor, Ruth.

Wow, those guys worked fast, they hadn't even been at the party for ten minutes and one of them was already scoring.

Mary couldn't see much of Ruth, her body was hidden from view by the large back of the man, but as she watched for a second she saw Ruth's legs twitching. With pleasure she assumed, again.

With a tinge of jealousy, she checked the boxes of beer and wine and then retreated out of the kitchen to leave the love birds alone. She had to see to her other guests and make sure they were getting what they deserved.

The kitchen door closed silently, Mary having returned to the party.

Across the kitchen, Ruth's legs continued to twitch. But not with pleasure, like Mary thought. If Mary had taken a closer look, she would have been shocked to see the ghoul holding Ruth's now lifeless body in its hands, while its teeth continued to chew on her throat.

Its mouth was covered in blood while it continued to feed, the parasites already infecting the corpse of Ruth.

Ten minutes past, with the ghoul devouring a huge chunk of Ruth's neck and shoulder, when Ruth's eyes snapped open again.

The whites of her eyes now tinted red from the alien toxins in her system, Ruth stumbled away from the ghoul.

Her head leaned at an unnatural angle thanks to the ghoul eating most of the muscle and tissue.

After a few moments to get her balance, Ruth turned for the kitchen door. The world was now sideways, her head swinging back and forth on her shoulder, but she'd adjust given time.

For now she was hungry and knew what she needed was on the other side of the door.

Mary moved amongst her guests, only pausing long enough to say a quick hello and then moving on.

She frowned when she looked at her rug in the corner of the living room. One of the new guests, one of the fellows in a zombie costume, had spilled red wine all over himself and it had then dripped onto the carpet. She was just about to go over to him, when she heard another scream from the far end of the house, by the kitchen.

Moving through the people and muttering apologies for bumping them, she made her way back through the house. Finally through the gauntlet, she stopped in astonishment when she saw what had caused the screaming.

Ruth had just walked out of the kitchen and she didn't look at all well. In fact, if Mary could be totally honest, well, Ruth looked dead.

And not just a little dead, but a lot dead. As in, there is no way that bitch should be walking around.

Bob ran up to her, asking her what had happened, if she was alright. Ruth just stared at him for a second, as if she was trying to make up her mind what to do.

Her mouth opened and nothing but a dry rasping sound came out, barely audible over the music from the other room.

Then Ruth smiled and her head swung back and forth on what was left of her neck.

Behind Ruth someone threw up, their stomach contents winding up on Mary's new Berber rug. But that was the least of Mary's concerns for the moment.

Before anybody could even move, Ruth had moved her body closer to Bob and her mouth had clamped down on his upper arm.

The man yelled at the top of his lungs, while he desperately tried to extricate himself from the crazy woman who used to be his mistress. But Ruth was having none of it. Her teeth squeezed tighter, the flesh ripping and the blood flowing into her mouth.

The viscous fluid revitalized her, prompting her to squeeze even more. Bob was screaming like an opera singer by now, his face contorted in pain.

Some of the guests had finally come to their senses and jumped onto Ruth, trying to pry her off poor Bob. After a few heaves, Ruth's jaw was disengaged from the arm it was so fond of.

A two inch round chunk of flesh was missing from Bob's arm, the man placing his hand over the wound and then running into the kitchen and out the back door.

His screams followed him long after he'd left, while two of the guests had a handle on Ruth.

With a snapping of jaws, she kept trying to sink her teeth into anyone stupid enough to get too close to her.

Mary heard her husband pushing through the crowd, his deep voice cutting through the other voices.

"Excuse me, please, excuse me, please. Come on, man, get the hell out of the way," Toby said, finally making it to his wife's side.

"Jesus, you can't move in here. Would someone please tell me what the hell is going on?" He asked the crowd of people surrounding Ruth.

One of the guests spoke up, a small man in a bright-yellow banana costume.

"No one really knows Toby, Ruth went fuckin crazy and took a bite out of Bob."

"What, that's ridiculous." Then he got a good look at Ruth.

"Holy shit, what the fuck happened to her?" He asked, his voice going up in pitch on the last word.

"No one knows, honey, we should call the police or an ambulance or something, although I think it's a little late for that," Mary said, watching Ruth warily. "You two, whatever you do, please don't let her go," Mary said to the two guests holding Ruth.

They nodded, already planning on holding the crazy woman with the sagging head.

Another guest spoke up. "I already tried the police, but all I get is a busy signal," the disembodied voice said.

Then another voice said the same thing with cell phone in hand.

"Maybe we should bring her to the hospital ourselves," Mary suggested.

Toby was about to answer her when a high-pitched scream cut through the chatter, coming from the other end of the house.

Almost everyone piled through the house to see what had happened, Toby pushing and shoving to be first in line. It was his house, for God's sake; he should see what was happening first.

A moment later, he wished he could take that back.

On the floor was one of the late arrivals dressed as a zombie. Under the man was one of Toby's guests.

The guest didn't look well, actually she was dead. More than half her throat had been torn out, her carotid artery sending blood spewing across the room to spray the once white walls of his Victorian house.

The music had been turned off now and the slurping sounds could be clearly heard over the mumbling of the guests.

With a roar, Toby grabbed the man and tore him off the poor woman under him. His nose was assailed by the smell and Toby idly wondered if his wife had let in a homeless man; although that wasn't really a problem in the suburbs of Boston. Maybe closer to the city, but not this far north.

Brushing the thought aside as irrelevant, Toby let the man fall to the living room rug.

"What the fuck's the matter with you? Are you some kind of a cannibal?" He asked the man.

The man just grinned, his eyes flaring red. Toby got a better look at the man now, but couldn't see much with all the rotting flesh for makeup the guy was wearing.

It would be hard to give the police a description of this murderer if he couldn't see what was under his mask.

"You two; get a hold of him," Toby said to a couple of large men who were standing by the man on the floor.

They picked him up and held him while Toby moved closer.

"Now, let's see what's under that mask, shall we?" He said, moving closer.

Reaching out to grab a piece of mask, he had to hold his breath.

"Christ, this guy reeks!" Toby exclaimed.

"Yeah, no shit," one of the men holding the ghoul said.

Toby had a handful of mask now, just below the chin, so he pulled back with all his strength. With a ripping sound the mask came clean off.

But instead of seeing the white or black face of a man, all they saw was the white and red skull of a corpse.

The skull glistened in the fluorescent lights of the room, bits of gore dropping to the rug. The mouth opened and grinned, looking like something out of anyone's worst nightmare.

The two men on the side of the zombie were so shocked they pushed him away.

The ghoul went flying across the room and fell on Mary's mother-in-law.

The zombie barely hesitated and with teeth flashing in the light, it dove in for the kill.

A mouth with no lips ripped into the flesh of Toby's mother, the woman screaming and hitting her attacker, but to no avail.

By the time Toby had made it to her and pulled the ghoul away, it was already too late.

Her wound was only superficial, but her heart had finally given out at the shock of being eaten alive. A massive coronary rocked her body and she was dead only moments after the zombie bit her.

The ghoul may not have done much damage to her body, but the parasites infecting the walking corpse had already transferred to Toby's mother and were already feeding and generating the chemicals that would soon bring his mother back from the dead.

Unaware of all this, Toby leaned over his mother with tears in his eyes.

Then he stood up and walked over to the zombie. With hate in his eyes he punched it in the face.

The zombie went down to the floor, the two men holding it letting go.

But Toby didn't stop. He was blinded by rage, stepping over to the zombie and kicking it in the face.

Teeth shattered, falling to the rug, followed by bits of red. Toby didn't stop there, though. Before the zombie could pick itself up, he kicked it again and again. When his foot was tired, he leaned down on one knee and started to punch it in the face until his knuckles were bloody and sore.

Finally, with his rage exhausted, he stood up and went to sit on the couch. His wife came over and sat next to him, comforting him even though deep in her heart she was glad the old bitch was finally dead.

Another scream came from another part of the house and several guests went to investigate.

Not Toby and Mary, though.

The two of them stayed on the couch, other problems not an issue for the moment.

Toby's mother's real name was Margaret, but everyone called her Meg.

Meg was very dead, lying on the once white carpet of her son's house.

But inside her body, the parasites were doing their thing, feeding on the meat inside her and returning the favor with toxins that were already reviving dead tissue.

While the guests wandered around talking together, no one noticed when Meg's eyes snapped open, her once blue eyes now tinted red.

Her wound still oozed blood, but it was a minor inconvenience to the old woman.

Her mouth cracked into a grin, showing the state of the art dentures she'd paid for with some of the life insurance money she'd received when her own husband had died five years before. Placing a hand under her, she pushed herself to a sitting position, eyes searching for just the right meal.

From across the room, she spotted her prey, her dislike for the woman carrying over to her now waking death...Mary.

Meg could already taste the flesh of the woman who had taken her son from her.

With a creaking of joints the old woman stood on unsteady feet. Slowly walking over to the couch, she had to resist the urge to bite all the warm bodies surrounding her. But she knew what she wanted, patiently waiting while she moved across the room.

Sitting on the couch, neither Toby nor Mary realized what was heading their way.

Mary was just about to get up and get her husband some ice for his hand, when she gazed up into the face of death itself.

Meg stood in front of her, and with Mary sitting, she felt like the old woman was ten feet tall.

Drool leaked from the corner of her mouth and with a twist of a cruel smile the old woman attacked.

Mary raised her hands to fend the old woman off. While the guests around her screamed and fought to get out of the way of another mad woman, Toby rose from the couch and pulled his mother off his wife.

"Oh my God, Mom, you're alive!" Toby screamed, his mother wiggling in his arms to get loose.

Meg kept shifting position in his arms until she was facing her son.

Toby looked into her face, his own face was ecstatic that his mother wasn't dead. Then she looked up into his face.

Toby gazed into her eyes, the red tint of the orbs giving her a devilish appearance.

He let her go and backed up a step, not quite comprehending what was going on. His mother was standing in front of him, but she wasn't acting normal.

Had she gone crazy like the other guests appeared to be doing?

"Mom, it's me, your son, Toby," he said, hoping to reason with her.

"Toby, get away from her, she's crazy!" Mary pleaded from across the room. All around them guests were leaving. From the back of the house more screaming and yelling could be heard.

Mary looked around. What the hell was going on tonight? Had everyone gone crazy? She thought.

Toby wouldn't give up. Looking down at his mother, he tried one more time.

Placing his hands on her shoulders he said: "Mom, are you all right? Do you want to go to the hospital?"

Meg just hissed and sank her teeth into his left arm, blood spurting into her mouth. Toby let out a yell that overrode every other voice in the house. Pushing his mother away, he stared in shock at his arm.

"What the fuck, Mom? I can't believe you just did that," he said, watching his mother warily.

Meg had stumbled backwards, but had regained her balance, and with a snarl, she lunged for her son again.

Toby didn't think about what he did next. If he did, he probably wouldn't have done what happened next. With Meg moving through the space separating the two of them, Toby brought back his right arm and with his hand curled into a fist, punched his mother right in the face.

The moment he did it, he regretted it, watching her fall to the floor with a broken neck.

"Oh God, Mom! I'm so sorry!" He screamed, moving to her side.

"I'm not," Mary mumbled from across the room.

Meg was sprawled across the carpet, her head bent at an odd angle. Toby knew before he even picked her up that he'd broken her neck. She was over eighty, after all.

Picking her up, her body slumped in his arms; he tried to come to grips with the fact that he had just killed his mother, when she turned to look at him.

Her head wouldn't move the way she wanted it to, thanks to the broken neck, but she was still able to take a bite out of his.

Her arms wrapped around his neck, and from a distance it looked like a son was carrying his mother to the couch, she in a loving embrace with her son.

Toby screamed again, throwing Meg away from him, but her teeth had sunk in pretty good, and when Toby threw her to the couch, she ripped half his throat out, blood spraying everywhere.

Toby stood there for a second, shock setting in, while his life's blood pumped out onto the once white carpet.

He placed a hand over his wound, but the blood still spurted through his fingers.

In the back of his mind, where reason still existed, he realized his mother had just ripped his throat out and now he was going to bleed to death in the middle of his living room.

Sitting down on the floor, he started to feel really tired and decided he would just close his eyes for a few minutes. Then he'd get up and take care of his neck wound.

Mary watched in stunned horror as her mother-in-law ripped her husband's throat out.

She called to him, but over the crowd, her voice was lost.

In the few seconds it took for her to reach her husband, it was already too late.

Before she could attend to him she had to stop Meg, who was even now crawling across the floor to finish off Toby.

Mary's eyes scanned the room, looking for something as a weapon, when she spotted the lamp on the end table. Before she realized what she was doing, she had grabbed the lamp and smashed it into Meg's face.

Meg went down hard onto the floor, where she twitched, struggling to get up.

Mary watched the old woman in horror.

The bitch just wouldn't stay down.

A few feet away from Mary were bookends she and Toby had purchased when they had gone antiquing one Sunday last fall. Her mind flashed to how heavy they were, and how she'd complained about carrying them around the bazaar for the day.

With a furtive glance over her shoulder to Meg, she grabbed a bookend.

Before she could change her mind, she ran at Meg, raising the bookend over her head and then with all her might, brought it straight down onto the old woman's head.

Meg's head split like a ripe melon, blood and gore spreading across the carpet, the material quickly soaking up the blood like a sponge.

Mary stood there heaving, trying to understand what she had just done.

Inside her head, the homemaker part of her was wondering how the hell she was going to get that stain out of the rug.

She let the bookend fall to the carpet, only then did she turn to her husband.

He was dead, no question. She felt for a pulse, but there was none.

With tears in her eyes, she stood up on shaky legs.

From across the room, a high-pitched scream snapped her out of her stupor, survival mode kicking in just a little.

Turning to the sound of the scream, she saw one of the zombies she'd let in late to the party. He was on top of a woman with his head down against her throat. Mary watched the zombie while it continued to eat the hapless woman, and after another second, her screams faded away with her life.

Becoming more aware of her surroundings, she now noticed there were bodies everywhere, scattered across her house. In a daze she walked into the kitchen and the scream froze in her throat.

Lying across the kitchen table was the man in the banana costume. Half his face was gone as well as a large chunk of his throat. His blood covered the kitchen table, where it then spilled over to fall in a spreading pool onto the imported Italian tile, a mosaic pattern appearing on the floor. Mary noticed the white grout was changing to red from the blood and wondered how she was going to get it clean.

The sliding glass doors to her right led to the backyard, and when she looked outside, she saw prone bodies sprawled on her lawn, while other people were on top of them.

Muffled cries of pain drifted through the tempered glass.

Mary's mind was slowly going, her grasp on reality slipping away with every second.

Whatever was happening tonight was too much for her to take and she was slowly building to a mental breakdown.

She backed out of the kitchen, moving through the kitchen door and back to the living room.

The only people left in her house were either dead, dying or being eaten.

She counted about twenty bodies spread out across the floor and furniture as she made her way through her house.

Returning to her husband's side, she knelt down next to him. With tears in her eyes she picked up his hand.

Grief overwhelmed her and she began to cry harder, never noticing Ruth crawling towards her, as her eyes were facing the floor in sadness.

The front door was open, the sounds of a town gone mad drifting into the living room.

Car alarms, sirens and yelling floated into her house, but she barely noticed, overwhelmed by her grief.

Slowly Ruth moved closer, her mouth dripping blood onto the carpet from a previous kill.

Then Mary's face perked up.

Toby's hand had twitched while she was holding it.

Maybe he wasn't dead, maybe he'd just passed out?

Her face lightened when she saw his head moving slowly from side to side, a low moan escaping his lips.

"Oh my God. Baby? Can you hear me? It's Mary," she said, tears of happiness now flowing freely down her cheeks.

Ruth was only a few feet behind her now, the dead woman already tasting the warm flesh that would soon be in her mouth.

So far, Mary was oblivious to the danger she was in.

Mary leaned helped Toby come to a sitting position, cradling his head in her arms.

"Don't worry, honey, you'll be fine. I'll call for help and then everything will return to normal, you'll see," she crooned, while rocking him back and forth.

Ruth was ready to pounce, the dead woman raising herself to her knees so she could force Mary to the floor and then attack her.

Mary was oblivious, her eyes only for her husband.

Sitting on the floor, she looked into her husband's face.

His eyelids were fluttering open!

Thank God, she thought. He's going to live!

Then she paused in mid-thought, looking into his now open eyes.

Where they were once a light shade of brown, they were now a dark red.

He glared up at her, his eyes seeing right through her.

He raised himself higher off the floor, opened his mouth as wide as he could, and sank his teeth into her throat.

Before Mary could scream in shock and pain, Ruth pounced on her from behind, the man and woman attacking Mary with teeth and nails.

Mary struggled for a few moments until shock set in from her already massive wounds. While her husband and neighbor continued to feed on her dying body, Mary had one last thought.

Her last fleeting thought was for her daughter, Kim. She was still outside somewhere, and if what was happening to her party was happening to the town, as well, she could only pray to God with her last breath that her child would survive the chaos.

Fifteen minutes later, Mary's house was empty. The bodies the ghouls had fed on now turning into the undead themselves.

With no food around them, they shuffled out of the house to find fresh meat.

At the end of the street ghouls wandered aimlessly.

On the sidewalk, near a mailbox were two zombies that had once resided in the quaint Victorian at the end of the block

A yellow and white cat was the only witness to the surreal scene playing out on this quiet rural street. The cat watched as the ghoul couple stumbled onto the sidewalk, the bodies not moving as well as before.

In the light of the moon the undead group turned to look at the cat.

Mary and Toby's eyes glowed red in the gloom of the night. The cat hissed once, sensing something was off, and then ran into the bushes, to be lost from sight.

On the street, the walking corpses continued on, looking for more prey.

Chapter 5

Officer Rick Johnson leaned against the streetlight and sucked in the night air.

Looking around, he was relieved to see the street was clear.

He had been running for almost an hour, his chest tight with pain from the exertion.

Rick had been a policeman for almost three weeks to the day, and was not prepared for the shit that was going down.

He had been on an easy detail tonight. Just stand around and keep an eye on the block party.

Not as much fun as chasing down all the kids who would try to raise hell tonight, but still a comfy assignment.

Then he'd received a call of a hit and run, not more than ten minutes from his position. Even though every man was working on Halloween, they were still spread thin, what with all the fights and mischief kids would get up to on this one day a year when it seemed it was okay to be bad.

So he had been dispatched to the scene.

When he'd arrived, everything had begun by the book.

Until one of the paramedics had been attacked and then a bunch of crazies had come from out of nowhere and attacked them all.

He'd called for backup and in less than five minutes, two more squad cars had come to his rescue...sort of.

The crazies had come out of the shadows and had attacked the paramedics.

Rick was scared out of his mind, but enough of his training remained for him to remember to draw his weapon. He had been assigned a .45 pistol, which was fine with him. He wasn't a big man and anything bigger would have looked stupid on his hip.

Like in one of those old westerns where the cowboy wore a cannon strapped to his leg.

After telling the driver of the Honda to beat it and with the paramedics screaming for help, he'd yelled to the group of crazies that if they didn't stop, he'd shoot.

He was totally ignored. After the second warning he had decided he no other choice, and just like they taught him at the academy, he spread his legs and aimed for a shoulder or a leg; whatever was easiest.

He fired a round at one of the zombies who at the moment was chewing on a paramedic's arm.

The bullet struck the target in the shoulder.

In the dark, with nothing but a streetlamp to see by, he couldn't tell if his shot was true.

It sure didn't look it. The man was going about his business as if nothing had happened.

Rick fired again, this time aiming for the meaty part of a thigh. Once again, the man was struck, but acted as if he didn't feel it. With sweat dripping down his face, he used his arm to soak up the excess perspiration and tried to decide what to do.

His heart jumped in his throat when some of the killers turned and began walking towards him. Swallowing hard, he was about to start firing when his backup pulled up. With the sound of sirens and car doors slamming, three more men and one woman officer ran to him.

"What the fuck is going on here?" A Sergeant said to Rick, with fire in his eyes.

The night had slowly gone to shit and this was the icing on the cake.

"Hell if I know. These guys came out of nowhere with masks on and started attacking the paramedics. But get this; the crazy bastards ate them!" Rick said, barely believing what he had just said; and he'd seen it with his own eyes.

The Sergeant started giving orders and the policemen set up a firing line, while the zombies continued forward.

The Sergeant had his weapon out; Rick was pretty sure it was a .38 Smith and Wesson. The Sergeant yelled to the approaching zombies.

"Attention! Lay down on the ground now or we will open fire! Do not come any closer. We will use deadly force if provoked!"

The zombies didn't even slow, their eyes flaring red in the gloom of the street.

When they were no more than a few feet away, the Sergeant gave the order to open fire. He knew it wasn't the right thing to do, as the approaching zombies had no apparent weapons, but hell, they'd just ripped two men apart and eaten them. He'd like to see the jury that would convict him and his men for wrongful deaths.

Gritting his teeth, he released his safety on his weapon. All right, if that was how it was going to be, then so be it.

In a rich, baritone voice he yelled: "Open fire!"

The next second the street was lit up with weapon's fire as the police shot down what they thought was a band of crazies.

Bullets penetrated dry skin, most just going through the frail bodies like paper.

A few bullets hit more vital areas, causing some limbs to be blown off and fall to the street.

Only one ghoul went down for good and it was Rick who had made the shot.

He had been aiming for the chest of a zombie closest to him and had shot it right where he'd wanted it. When the gun had risen in his hand from the kick, he'd pulled the trigger again, although not really meaning too. The second bullet had hit the zombie in the face, blowing the fragile skull to pieces.

The ghoul had fallen to the street and remained still, but before Rick could shoot any others, the crazies had been on them.

They had shrugged off the bullets like some kind of ghouls and now while he watched, his fellow officers were fighting for their lives.

At the moment, he was the only one not being attacked, but turning around, he saw that was about to change.

Two of the crazies with masks that looked like they came out of the best zombie movie he'd ever seen, were circling around the squad car to get him.

He fired once at the closest attacker and his jaw dropped when there was nothing more than a puff of dust from where the bullet hit it in the chest.

That's when he decided to cut and run. Looking around, he saw his fellow officers on the ground and some of the others were being dragged away back to the lawn of the mortuary.

He figured if he stayed, all that would happen is that he'd end up like the rest.

He checked his squad car, but it was on the other side of a group of crazies. He'd never make it before they reached him.

So he decided to just run.

Holstering his weapon, he backed up and started to run down the street, heading back to the main road. Craning his neck over his shoulder, he was relieved to see he wasn't being followed. He kept running, his boots echoing off the pavement until he was far away from the carnage.

Fifteen minutes later, he took a breather. He could smell smoke, but not fireplace smoke, no, this smelled like a house was burning.

A moment later the sounds of sirens came to him, drifting over the houses.

Looking into the night surrounding him, he couldn't tell where it was from, the smoke blending with the night.

Spotting a phone booth, he ran to it and dived inside, closing the door behind him. After fishing out fifty cents, he called the police station to report in. All he got was a busy signal.

He waited five more minutes and tried again, with the same results.

The sound of crashing, tearing metal, signifying a car crash, penetrated through the phone booth's doors.

He looked up, but to him it sounded like it came from a few streets over.

Deciding to hoof it back to the station, he left the phone booth be-hind and began walking.

A scream floated on the night air followed by a car alarm.

What the hell was going on around here? This was Wakefield, Mass., not Beirut!

He continued moving, it was at least another mile and a half until he made it to the station. With his hand on his weapon for peace of mind, he continued up the deserted street.

*   *   *

Two streets over, a lone ghoul wandered into a backyard. A large dog was tethered to a dog house. The animal was a mix of Doberman and German shepherd.

The second the dog saw the shambling form, it began to bark, the ghoul continuing forward. The dog wasn't human, but it would do to satisfy its hunger in a pinch.

Without hesitation, the walking corpse knelt down and bit into the side of the dog.

With a yelp of pain the dog bit the zombie back, but the fight was doomed from the start.

Before long the animal was dead and the zombie was feeding on its flesh.

Suddenly, the back door to the house banged open and a middle-aged man in a pair of worn boxer shorts and a t-shirt ran out screaming for it to get the hell away from his dog.

The man grabbed the ghoul by the scruff of the old suit it had been buried in and tossed the corpse away. After a moment, the ghoul got back to shaky feet and faced the balding man. The home-owner's face went slack when he saw what was standing in front of him

Before the man could fight or run away, the ghoul pushed the man to the ground with itself on top, trapping him on the mostly dead and yellow lawn.

Teeth sank into the man's throat, and moments later the dirt was wet with blood as the zombie was gorged on what it really wanted... human meat.

Next to the killer and victim, the dog twitched on the ground.

The worms were doing their part, and man or animal; it made no difference to them.

The dog's eyes flared red, and a moment later it stood up on unsteady legs.

Its fur was matted in blood and half its right shoulder was torn apart as the dog pulled on its leash to free itself.

Feeling no pain, it didn't take long for the leash to pull from its moorings, and the dog ran out of the yard, leash trailing behind it.

It ran down the street searching for food, tongue hanging out. Hearing noises from the next street over, it turned and shot off into a yard, to be lost in the darkness.

Behind the escaping dog, on the front lawn of its old home, the ghoul continued feeding on its master.

Chapter 6

John parked his Honda next to the security pickup truck near the front door of the office building where he presently worked security on the night shift.

Stepping out of his car, he gazed up at the night sky. In the distance, the sky was a little lighter and the smell of smoke assailed his nose.

There was a fire somewhere in the city, he thought, turning to walk to the front door. He hadn't even pulled the door open when Tod pushed through the doors, throwing the master keys at him.

"About damn time, you're two hours late," he snapped.

John scratched his head "Yeah, sorry about that. On the way here I hit a..."

Tod cut him off. "You know what, John? I really don't give a shit. I guess I should thank you for coming in anyway, though."

The man already had his jacket on and his car keys were in his hand.

"Well, I'm outta here. You should check out the news. There's some weird shit happening tonight; bunch of people going crazy and attacking people. Figures, though, it is Halloween, after all... night, John," Tod said, not waiting for an answer and walking out the door.

John stood there and watched Tod jump into his old Buick and with the revving of his engine, backed up and shot off down the driveway.

John looked around the lobby for a moment, then locked the front doors and got settled for the night.

It had been quite an adventure getting here tonight, but he was here now, so he might as well relax.

* * *

After double checking the doors to the building, John sat down in the chair at the desk situated in the middle of the lobby.

There were a few security monitors on the left side of the desk showing the loading dock and the front and rear entrances of the building.

The building he was in contained twelve floors. Not much compared to the high-rises in Boston, but still not too bad for the suburbs.

The late shift wasn't so bad, actually. Usually he got a few hours of sleep in after he did rounds of the floors, making sure there were no pipes leaking or fires in the offices.

The pay wasn't that good, but then, he didn't have to work that hard, so it averaged out.

On the desk in the lobby was a small nine inch black and white television.

The reception wasn't great, but he was usually able to pull in a few channels.

Channel 25 and 56 were the best for late night comedy reruns like Cheers and Taxi. Usually he was able to get 4, 5 or 7, as well, but the picture was always full of snow and squiggly lines. It always reminded him of when he was a kid and he tried to sneak a peek at the scrambled porn channels on his parent's television.

Tonight he had decided to suffer with the fuzzy reception, so he could find out what was going on in town and the world, so he set the tuner on 5.

After playing with the antenna for a good two minutes, he was able to get a clear enough picture to see by.

He didn't like what he saw.

An anchorman for ABC news was talking about exactly what Tod had said, while pictures of fires and riots were seen in a smaller picture behind him.

According to the anchorman, riots had happened all across the United States and in some countries overseas.

People were urged to stay in their homes and not go to work tomorrow, at least until the police and National Guard could regain control.

"Great," he mumbled to himself. Did that mean that no one would be here in the morning to relieve him? How long was he supposed to stay here?

Sighing, he decided it didn't really matter now. He'd worry about it in the morning.

Picking up the master keys from the desk and whistling a tune, he decided to go do his rounds; the rest of the shit would work itself out eventually.

He just had to be patient.

*   *   *

Kim had been running for what felt like hours, but she had finally made it to her home street.

People were out, wandering around, and she had to constantly run away from them. They kept trying to grab her and their faces looked weird.

They all had the same thing wrong with their eyes, just like the crazy people at the mortuary.

She had hoped to find a cop, but had been unsuccessful.

About ten minutes ago, she had seen flashing lights coming towards her and had tried to wave the cruiser down, but it had just blown by her, ignoring her.

Disappointed, she had continued home.

Now she was on her street and it looked really weird. Some of the houses had their doors open and after checking her watch, which read 1:00 a.m., she knew that wasn't right.

Then she saw her neighbor, Ruth, slowly walking down the sidewalk like she was drunk or ill.

Kim ran over to her and before she was even ten feet from the older woman, Kim knew there was definitely something wrong with her.

Her head was at an incredibly unnatural angle and the front of her costume was covered in what Kim had to assume was blood.

Kim began to back away from the deformed woman, but not before another person came up on her from behind. Just before the person could grab her, she jumped out of the way, dead arms grabbing air. Kim took one look at the other person, red eyes clearly visible in the gloom of the street and ran away.

She continued to run, dodging the few people on the street, until she'd made it to her house. She noticed the front door was open, so she dashed inside, slammed the door closed and locked it.

Scanning the room, she couldn't believe what she saw. The once white rug was now mostly red and as she walked around on her way to the kitchen, she saw pieces of skin and gore. Her nose wrinkled from the stench of death.

"Mom, Dad?" She called, not really expecting an answer.

The phone was on the floor, so she picked it up and checked for a dial tone.

Upon hearing one, she dialed the police again, but just heard the same message droning on. Disgusted, she placed the phone back on the end table and walked into the kitchen.

Her eyes opened wider when she saw blood everywhere. The floor was covered in a thin congealing layer of red and most of the walls, as well.

Where could all this blood have come from, and if it was real blood, where were all the bodies? And where were her parents? All these questions flooded through her mind in a flash.

Moving back to the living room, she noticed a pair of legs sticking out from behind the couch.

Walking as quietly as she could, she crept over and then looked around the couch to see her Grandma Meg's lifeless body.

Biting back a scream, she dashed upstairs to her bedroom, and after pushing the door open so hard the doorknob dented the wall behind it, she fell onto the bed and cried.

She cried for a good hour, thinking of her boyfriend and her other friends, now all dead, and for her Grandma, lying dead right below her bedroom.

She cried until the exhaustion of the night finally caught up to her and she fell asleep.

Her dreams were filled with red-eyed demons trying to kill her while she ran as fast as she could, trying to escape.

Eventually, her nightmares subsided, and she slept easier, although restless.

Outside her windows, the town of Wakefield was slowly being taken over by the undead, one person at a time.

Chapter 7

Rick's feet hurt.

He'd been walking for twenty minutes with boots that were two sizes too big.

He had received the wrong size when he'd been issued them and hadn't had a chance to get new ones.

Man, was he paying for it now. His right foot had to have at least two good size blisters from where the loose leather kept rubbing his ankle.

Trying to ignore the pain, he trudged on.

He had just made it to Wakefield Center; the police station only a few streets away, when he spotted a small group of people shuffling up the sidewalk across the street.

Knowing it was dangerous to be out with killers on the loose; he figured he should warn them to get home.

Starting to walk closer to the group, he paused when the first person in line walked under a streetlight. The yellow glow of the lamp gave the face of the man an even pastier look as the group continued forward, not yet noticing him.

Rick decided he'd give it a second before calling to them, just in case.

Ducking behind a car parked along the sidewalk, he hunched down and watched the slow moving group.

When they were directly across the street from him, with the light from a hardware store illuminating them as clear as day, Rick's eyes opened as wide as they could upon seeing the condition of the four pedestrian's bodies.

There were two men and two women in the group, their pale bodies showing various mortal wounds.

The first man in line had half his throat ripped out, while the woman directly behind him was missing her nose and had a good size chunk of her left arm missing. But it was the last guy in line that had Rick trying to keep the rest of his dinner down.

The front of the man's chest was a gaping wound and while he walked, pieces of his insides were falling out to land on the sidewalk with a slapping sound.

Across the street, with the downtown center being empty, the echo of that sound floated to him clear as day.

Rick had to close his eyes for a moment until his rumbling stomach subsided.

From his hiding spot, Rick watched the four people that sure as hell should not be walking around turn a corner and walk up a side street.

If they continued on their present course they would reach North Street and the T- Purple line, train station in a few minutes.

That was fine with Rick as he wanted to go the other way.

Poking his head up over the car he was behind, he saw it was clear and while still crouching low, ran across Main Street.

Reaching the corner, he peeked around it to make sure the next street was clear and then took off at a jog.

If all went well, he would be at the police station in a few minutes and everything would be fine.

*   *   *

With the police station in sight, Rick slowed down to a walk. Sweat was pooling in the middle of his back as he quickly crossed the street.

It was an unseasonable sixty degrees out; another Indian summer, just like the year before.

The smell of burning wood drifted to his nose, stronger now. Moving to the steps of the police station, he idly wondered if there was anyone fighting the fire.

He ran up the steps, taking them two at a time, pushing through the double doors at the top.

Stepping inside, he was immediately aware of the emptiness. With the exception of the phones ringing, there didn't seem to be anyone around.

Maybe they were in back, Rick thought.

Walking behind the front desk, he moved through the maze of desks, until he was at the back of the station.

He poked his head into the small break room, but frowned when it was empty.

Strange, he didn't think everyone would leave no matter how bad it got out in the town. The phones hadn't stopped ringing, so Rick decided to answer one.

"Wakefield police, this Officer Johnson, this call is being recorded," he stated into the phone.

"Oh my God, thank you for answering, I've been trying forever; you've got to help me! My husband was attacked in the backyard by some crazy person and now he's trying to get me!" A voice pleaded.

"Wait a minute, miss, now slow down. Who's attacking who?" Rick asked.

"My husband is, he's crazy now, too, and he's trying to kill me. I've locked myself in the bathroom, but he's beating on the door. I don't know how long it will hold. Please come quick!" The frightened voice pleaded.

"All right, miss, where do you live? I'll see what I can do," Rick said calmly, falling back on his training.

"I'm at 1352..." Suddenly there was a loud crashing on the phone, followed by a high pitched scream. "Oh my God, he got in! The lock broke!" The woman screamed. "Please help me!"

Then the sounds of a scuffle, followed by more screams poured through the receiver.

"Hello, hello, are you there, miss?" Rick asked, anxiously.

Nothing, the phone had gone dead.

Rick placed the phone down, despite the fact the switchboard was lit up like a Christmas tree.

After a second to get himself together, he answered another call.

This one was from a man who said there were ten people congregating outside his living room window in the street. They appeared to be beating up another man who was lying very still on the ground. The weird thing was it looked like the man on the ground was being eaten. The man on the phone wanted to know what kind of a sick Halloween prank these people were playing at and what the police were going to do about it.

"Look, sir," Rick said. "I think you should stay in your house. If the people aren't threatening you, then leave them alone. There's some strange shit going down tonight and we don't have the manpower to handle it."

"That's your answer? Well then screw you. I was in WW2 and I know how to handle myself. I'll take care of those punks myself."

"No, sir, you don't want to do that, stay in your home," Rick pleaded, but it was too late; the line had gone dead.

Rick sat still for another moment, then pressed another lit-up button on the phone and answered another call.

The next call and the one after that were all the same. There were people trespassing or attacking others in the streets and the police were needed. Only Rick didn't know where everyone was.

After the twentieth call he stopped answering the phone. What was the point? It wasn't like he could single handedly help everyone.

He'd been on the job for a little over three weeks, for God's sake!

The dispatch desk was near the back and he walked over to the radio, hoping to hear something on the air.

He began calling some of the other units he knew were out on patrol tonight, but all he received was dead air.

What the hell was going on? Where were the other cops?

He had no real idea what he was expected to do in a situation like this, so he decided to just sit tight and wait. Sooner or later someone should come back to the station.

Amidst the ringing phones, he put his head down and rested. It had been a long night. He had started his shift at 2:00 in the afternoon and now it was going on 1:30 in the morning. He was exhausted.

Despite the noise and the bright fluorescent lights, he soon drifted off into a restless slumber.

*   *   *

All across the United States, the dead were rising. Cemeteries were disgorging their dead residents by the thousands as the worms continued to feed on the lifeless bodies.

Emergency crews were arriving, but were soon overwhelmed by the horde of the undead. Then those victims would rise and join their undead brethren and attack others. On the east coast, with Halloween over, millions slept oblivious to what was happening.

Soon the moon dropped from the horizon and the sun began to rise. People woke to alarm clocks and hungry, crying babies.

Men and women got ready to go to work for another day, pouring themselves a cup of coffee and kissing husbands and wives goodbye.

Mothers got their children ready for school, yelling at them for eating Halloween candy for breakfast.

Another day was starting, no different from a thousand other days.

Except one very important difference.

The dead had risen...and they were hungry.

Chapter 8

George Mahoney shrugged into his jacket and picked up his cup of coffee from the small table near his front door.

Checking his wrist watch, he was pleased to see he was still on time for work.

He had heard the news reports when he'd woken up that morning about staying home and not going to work.

He chose to ignore it. He had a pile of paperwork to deal with when he got to the office this morning and he'd be damned if he was going to stay home.

Besides, the news always made things sound worse than they really were for better ratings. Just because a bunch of nuts were running around causing mayhem was no reason for him to hide in his house.

Pulling the door open, he slipped outside into the cool, crisp November morning.

There was a family of birds in the bare tree on his front lawn and he paused for just a second and listened to them chirping at each other.

Then he walked the ten feet to his car, pleased to see it had escaped the regular egging it received every Halloween.

Upon reaching his car he noticed his neighbor Wayne sitting on his front stairs with his newspaper dangling from one hand.

He and Wayne had just gotten over an argument about where the property line for their house was.

For the past three weeks they'd bickered about it until George had hired a surveyor. With the property line now clearly marked out in a line of sticks with red cloths hanging from them, George had thought the disagreement was over.

Before climbing into his car he called to Wayne, casually.

"Morning, Wayne, how was your Halloween?"

Wayne just sat there, ignoring him.

George waited for another half second and then said: "Screw it; you want to hold a grudge, then fine."

Aggravated that he was letting his neighbor get to him, he climbed into his car and backed out of the driveway. The whole time, Wayne just sat there, not moving a muscle, oblivious to George.

Once George had backed down his driveway, he headed off down Bennett Street to the stop sign at the end of the road.

If he'd taken a better look at Wayne, he might have noticed the left side of his shoulder and face, but it was blocked from George's view due to the angle of the driveway. If he had seen it, he would have noticed it was a bloody mess of torn and shredded flesh and small maggots could be seen wiggling around.

Earlier that morning, Wayne had gone out to get the newspaper, which was delivered right on time, despite the news warnings.

When he'd leaned down to pick it up a large dog had come out of the bushes from the house across the street, its red eyes flaring in the wan light of the rising sun. Before he could even scream, his throat had been ripped out, the dog then chewing on whatever was available.

A truck had driven down the road, the loud engine spooking the animal.

It had run away to find other food, leaving Wayne to bleed out in his driveway, his body hidden by the trash barrels.

Sometime later, Wayne had revived and had wandered back to his steps, where he had sat the rest of the morning, not quite used to being dead yet.

George had come and gone now, when behind him the front door opened. His wife stood there, looking perplexed.

"Wayne, honey, are you going to come back inside? You've been out there all morning. The news says its not safe outside," his wife said.

Wayne turned to look at her, the bloody side of his face and body facing her.

"Oh my God!" She screamed, running onto the front porch to help him.

"What happened to you, we have to call an ambulance," she said, helping him to his feet.

The man who was once Wayne didn't hesitate. With her neck not more than a few inches from his mouth, he sank his teeth into her flesh, ripping tendons and tissue.

His wife screamed, falling back into the house, while Wayne jumped on top of her, continuing to rip and chew, his bloodlust far from ending.

Her flailing legs pushed the front door closed with a slam, her husband never letting up.

Another commuter drove by the quaint, one-story house with the red blood stain on the driveway and front porch, unaware of what had just transpired.

*   *   *

George stopped his car as he approached an intersection. There were a bunch of people standing in the street blocking traffic.

On the other side of the street another car, a Volvo by the looks of it, had also stopped.

With horns blaring, both cars attempted to warn off the crowd.

George watched, while they ignored him and the Volvo, so he rolled down his window to yell at the nearest man's back.

"Hey, asshole, would you mind getting the hell out of the street. I'd like to get to work today," George snapped.

The man just stood there, his body seeming to sway like he was drunk.

Great, thought George. These people were leftover partiers from last night who haven't figured out that Halloween was over.

He saw movement in his rearview mirror. Turning, he saw three more people surrounding his car.

What the hell were these people doing? He thought.

Staring at the man's back, who he'd already yelled to, he tried again.

"Come on, buddy, get the hell out of the road or I'm gonna call the cops!" He yelled, threateningly. "Halloween's over and some of us have to go to work!"

That seemed to do it. The man turned around to face him and George's breath lodged in his throat.

The front of the man's shirt was ripped to shreds and pieces of his insides were hanging out of the open wound like a squished cherry pie.

With George frozen in fear, the man stumbled over to his car. From the other side of his car, someone else had opened his passenger side door and was even now reaching for him.

The woman now in his car had half her face missing and one eyeball hung from its socket by one tiny piece of gristle.

George watched the eye swing back and forth like a pendulum while the woman tried to grab his legs, despite his attempts to repeatedly kick her away.

He was doing a good job of fending her off when the ghoul with the open chest reached through the window and wrapped its hands around his neck, pulling him back against the door. The zombie was trying to pull him out the half open window but simple dynamics made that impossible. With hands wrapped around his throat and another crazy person reaching for him from inside the car, George valiantly fought for his life.

But it was a lost cause.

The woman in the car was able to get by his kicking legs and with his head pulled back against the window; she darted in, ripping the front of his throat out, like a Southerner eating ribs.

Blood sprayed from his severed jugular like a broken water fountain, covering the windshield and dashboard with blood.

With his last breath bubbling from his torn throat, he was able to see through a clear spot in the windshield. The same thing that was happening to him was happening across the road to the occupants of the Volvo. Then the blood dripped down more and covered the peephole on the windshield.

The woman ghoul continued to rip him apart, gorging herself on his flesh.

Mercifully, George had passed out from blood loss and was seconds away from death.

With the sounds of the dead gorging on their victims floating over the once quiet street, the birds in the nearby trees zipped by on their way to find food, uninterested in the machinations of man.

Chapter 9

Greg Daniels had been running all morning, unfortunately he wasn't in shape.

His morning had started like any other morning. He'd gotten up with the alarm clock blaring in his ear, then did the three S"s (shit, shower and shave) and then he'd had a breakfast of day old pizza.

Before leaving his house, he'd been pleased to see he was right on schedule.

He'd grabbed his coat, keys, and the lunch he'd made the night before and left the house for another exciting day in the world of office supply.

Walking down the street to the bus stop, he couldn't help but notice how weird it felt this morning on the street.

For one thing, there were almost no cars driving by him this morning and when he looked at the houses set back from the curb, he saw nothing but drawn shades and dark windows.

Had he missed something?

Despite last night being Halloween, he'd been exhausted. So, after placing a bowl filled with candy bars outside his door (to hopefully prevent his house from being bombarded with eggs from some disgruntled kid) he'd gone straight to bed, well before ten.

Now, while he was walking down the sidewalk, he couldn't help getting the chills. Something just wasn't right.

Six minutes later, he'd reached the empty bus stop, and while leaning against a light pole, figured he'd better have a smoke before the bus came.

Pulling out a pack of whatever generic brand had been on sale at the time he'd needed to buy more, he lit it up and let the smoke and nicotine fill his lungs.

Breathing out, the smoke drifting off lazily into the sky, he immediately felt better.

He couldn't get laid everyday, but at least he could have a cigarette.

Feeling a little better, he calmly watched a small group of people walking over to him from across the street.

The only thing was, from where they'd come from there was nothing else over there but the backyards of private homes.

There looked to be about five of them, all in different states of dress.

Maybe people that had stayed too long at a party last night and had slept it off on their hosts couch or floor?

When they were directly across the street from him, he saw all of them were covered in red paint.

A Halloween prank gone bad?

Taking a moment to look up the street, he frowned when he saw nothing. The street was empty. Where the hell was his bus? If it didn't show he was screwed, as he sure didn't have enough in his wallet for a cab.

The five people had started to cross the street and Greg watched them curiously.

When they were no more than eight feet away, Greg's jaw dropped, his cigarette falling to the gray cement of the sidewalk.

He'd seen costumes of zombies and vampires and the like, but he'd never seen them look so authentic; with the exception of a high budget movie.

"Wow, guys, those costumes are great, did you buy them or make them yourselves?" He asked, politely.

No one said anything.

He thought that was odd until it became odder.

The first guy in line grinned, his teeth covered in red as well, then without warning, the man lunged for Greg.

Instinctively, Greg jumped away, the man's hands reaching for empty air.

"Hey, what's your problem, man?" He asked; his feathers ruffled. The last thing he needed was to get into a fight with a bunch of drunken idiots.

Still, no one said anything. Suddenly the second person in the group, a young woman, tried to jump on him.

He deftly twisted out of the way, but was now on guard. The first guy was still on his side and looked like he might try something again.

"Look, fellas, I don't want no trouble. If you want I'll leave, okay?" He asked, trying to reason with them.

Until now, Greg just assumed he was dealing with a bunch of drunken assholes. That all changed when the last person in line shuffled to the front of the group.

The guys head was practically torn off, with nothing but a small piece of spine to hold it in place.

When the guy tried to talk, nothing but gurgles came out of the neck cavity.

Greg felt his breakfast wanting to make an appearance.

He'd seen costumes and he'd seen people from really bad car crashes and he was starting to think that guy wasn't wearing a costume.

The first ghoul grabbed his arm and Greg ripped it away from its grip. He started to back away from them, deciding it was a good time to make a strategic retreat, when a speeding car shot up the road.

It looked like two teenagers were in it as the car swerved to take out one of the guys in the group attacking him.

With the roar of the engine, the car hit one of the bodies head-on, flipping it into the air. It landed ten feet in front of Greg, the car never having slowed down. With a screech of brakes the car turned the corner at the end of the street and was gone, nothing but the echo of the revving engine and laughter following its passage.

"Holy shit," he screamed, not able to believe what he'd just witnessed.

Then the morning got even stranger. The ghoul that had flew through the air started to drag itself back to Greg and the others.

While he continued avoiding the other walking corpses, for whatever reason, none of them moved too fast, he watched while the shattered corpse continued to drag itself along the lawn and sidewalk of the house it had landed in front of.

Greg looked up as the front door to that same house flew open and a middle aged woman ran out onto the lawn; her hair curled up in rollers and a worn housecoat covering her ample frame.

"Oh my Lord, I saw that car. I can't believe that guy isn't dead. I've called for an ambulance, but the line is busy."

She ran to the crawling ghoul to try and help him. Leaning down to his face, she screamed when it grabbed her arm and pulled her to the sidewalk.

Greg watched in horror, not believing what he was seeing, as the man took a bite out of the woman's throat.

Her screams lasted for only a second, her life's blood squirting across her lawn.

Within less than a minute she'd bled out, the ghoul digging in with bloody teeth.

The slurping sound carried to Greg's ears and he definitely felt breakfast coming back up. At the same time the woman zombie lunged for him again, he shot vomit into her face. She immediately missed him and stumbled away, bits of pizza getting stuck in her eyes, impairing her vision.

Greg wiped his mouth and decided it was time to go. He still didn't quite get what was going on, but he'd just witnessed a murder and that was something he didn't need in his life right now.

Dodging one of the ghouls one final time, he took off at a run, dropping his lunch to the sidewalk as excess baggage.

There was another bus stop half a mile down the street; maybe that one would be a little quieter. With his nerves totally rattled, he jogged up the sidewalk, leaving the other people to feed on the middle-aged woman.

He felt bad, but what could he do? It's not like he was a cop or something.

Trying to assuage his troubled conscience, he continued jogging, leaving the visceral scene behind him.

Chapter 10

Instead of waking to her alarm clock, Kim Murphy was startled awake by the sound of screaming coming from the front of her house.

With her heart in her throat, and sleep still in her eyes, she stumbled to the bedroom window to see what was happening outside.

Her breathing stopped when she saw the grotesque tableaux taking place practically on her front lawn.

Their paperboy was lying in a pool of his own blood, the tires on his ten speed bike still spinning. There were two people on top of him, a man and a woman; and they appeared to be eating him.

As for the paperboy, well, he didn't seem to be moving.

The woman looked up at the house, perhaps sensing she was being watched, and Kim let out a gasp in surprise.

It was her Mom!

And she was eating the paperboy!

Kim watched in horror when her mom dove in for another bite of the paperboy; blood and entrails falling out of her teeth while she gorged herself.

The man turned his face enough for Kim to see him better, but he didn't look familiar.

Kim just stood at the window for a moment, watching the horrifying scene; a scene that could have come straight out of a low budget horror movie.

Then she dashed down the stairs to the front door, and after pulling it open, ran down the front walk to her mother.

"Mom!" She yelled. "What the hell are you doing?"

Mom glanced up at her daughter, but there was no sign of recognition in her cold, red eyes. Instead, she crawled away from the paperboy, to the delight of the male ghoul, who was now pleased he didn't have to share anymore. The dead woman started moving towards her daughter, on hands and knees like a baby.

Kim took two steps back, the creature in front of her may have looked like her mother, but a sixth sense told her what was inside her had changed.

"Oh my God, you're one of them," Kim gasped, thinking of the crazy people she'd seen at the mortuary; the one's that had killed Paul and Joey.

The sound of shoes clicking on the sidewalk made her turn to her left.

Stumbling down the sidewalk were three more people. Kim watched them for only a second, but it was clear to her they weren't normal either.

Continuing to back away from her mother, she turned and ran back into her house, slamming the door and locking it behind her.

She stayed there for a few minutes, her heart pounding a mile a minute. Her mind still trying to wrap itself around everything she'd seen, when the door jumped in its frame.

Her back was still leaning against it and she jumped away, screaming in a short, high pitched shriek, the banging continuing.

Slowly, with butterflies of fear in her stomach she went to the front bay window in the living room.

Peeking outside, she muffled another scream when she saw her mother as well as the other people she'd seen on the sidewalk, now banging on the front door of the house.

The front door had a six by ten decorative piece of stained, leaded glass by the doorknob and Kim jumped when it shattered, the fragments falling to the carpeted floor.

Dirty, bloody hands shot through the hole in the door, reaching for whatever they could find.

Kim backed away from the grasping hands, moving further into the house.

When her back hit the swinging kitchen door, she darted through it.

Another shriek left her lips at the sight that greeted her.

The sliding glass doors leading out to the backyard showed her three more crazy people milling about her yard.

When she shrieked, their heads turned to see her standing in the middle of the kitchen.

As one, the three ran at her, but bounced off the glass.

Shaking their heads in a daze, they climbed back to their feet and ran at the glass again with the same results.

Kim watched this, thanking God the glass was holding.

But for how long?

Her eyes darted around the room like a caged animal, until she spied her mother's car keys on their hook by the back door.

Like she was jumping for a life line, Kim ran across the kitchen, her shoes slipping on the congealed blood. Catching her balance, she grabbed the keys and then moved off to the door that led to their two car garage.

Hope filled her when she saw both of her parent's cars sitting quietly, nestled in their bays.

Shattering glass filled the kitchen and she turned to see the men had broken through the sliding glass doors and had started towards her.

With only one option, she darted into the garage, and with the horn sounding a gentle beep, beep, she turned off the car alarm to her mom's SUV.

Jumping in, she turned the ignition, the engine surging to life.

With the crash of the kitchen door, the men filed into the garage. Kim had already hit the remote for the garage door, and before it was even halfway up, she'd floored the gas pedal, the SUV shooting out of the garage like a rocket.

The luggage rack scraped the bottom of the garage door as the vehicle shot out of the structure and into the sunlit morning.

With tires screeching, she cut the wheel hard and took off down the street.

With a quick glance over her shoulder, she saw her mother and the others still banging on the front door of her house. Then she had to focus on her driving. The streets were a mess with abandoned cars and other people walking wherever they felt.

She slowed the SUV just a little while driving by an older woman in a housecoat.

When the woman was right at her window, Kim took a good look at her.

The woman's eyes were the same red color as the others she'd seen and her neck had a large red wound on it.

Small bubbles of blood came out of the wound to drip down onto her housecoat.

Kim shivered, watching. Then she turned the corner and headed down to Main Street. Once she reached the town square, she planned to cut across it and drive to the police station.

On her left, one of the houses was on fire, the flames reaching up to the clear, blue sky. Looking around, she didn't understand why the fire department wasn't trying to put out the blaze. Then she was past the burning house and other crazy things caught her attention.

With her heart in her throat, she swerved to avoid a Volvo in the street. It was sitting at the stop sign at the end of the road, but with the exception of blood covering the driver's door, the owner of the vehicle was gone.

Repressing an urge to scream, she continued deeper into town.

She knew that if she started screaming this time, it was highly doubtful she'd be able to stop.

Chapter 11

Greg slowed down when he reached the next bus stop, sharp pains shooting up his side the entire time.

"Christ, I need to give up the smokes," he muttered to himself.

He stood there alone, the only one on the street. Off in the distance, he could hear sirens and see smoke drifting over the houses.

Bending over with his hands on his knees, he breathed in deep, the cool November air chilling his throat.

When he finally had control of his breathing, he stood up and looked around again.

"Oh, shit," he said aloud

Six crazies had just turned the corner at the end of the street and were now moving straight towards him.

From where he stood, it was easy to see the signs that the teenagers down the street weren't normal. For one thing, normal people didn't walk around with their intestines dragging behind them nor did they function when their throat's were ripped out, which was the case with two of the teenagers. And they were all still wearing their Halloween costumes, although with a little more blood than from when they'd started out the night before. The cloth was torn and ripped; reminding him of what a bear attack would look like.

The teenagers were moving at a good speed and Greg realized if he didn't move now, they'd be on him in seconds.

His eye caught the house behind him, the front door looking as good a place as any to try to hide in.

Turning, he ran up the front walk and rang the bell multiple times. When only seconds had passed, he started banging on the door and ringing the bell again.

He saw a shadow move across the peephole in the door and a second later the door swung inward. Before Greg could do or say anything, a double barreled shotgun was shoved into his face.

Behind the weapon was a fat, bald guy with the hairiest chest Greg had ever seen.

"What the fuck do you want?" Fatty yelled.

"Help me, please, there's a bunch of psychos out here," Greg pleaded.

Fatty looked over Greg's shoulder, spotting the closing group.

"Yeah, I can see that. Looks like you're pretty well fucked. If I were you, I'd run."

"Run? Why won't you let me in so I can call the police or something?" Greg pleaded.

Fatty shook his head no, the shotgun never wavering.

"Sorry, pal, it's every man for himself. I've got just enough food for me and the phones are dead, so if I were you I'd start running because the only way you're getting into my house is over my dead body."

Greg stared at the man, stunned. How could this guy be so insensitive and selfish? Looking over his shoulder, Greg realized he had about thirty seconds to decide what to do, so with another brief look at the shotgun, he decided to leave.

Darting across Fatty's lawn and jumping the three foot fence into the neighbor's yard, he continued running, his feet hitting pavement again as he took off up the next street.

Behind him he heard a shotgun blast. Craning his head over his shoulder, he could hear fatty shooting the teenagers. Then he turned a corner and the sounds of the massacre began to fade away.

While Greg continued to run, the shotgun blasts echoed across the sky.

With the sounds of sirens in the distance, smoke filling the air and people shooting other people in the streets, Greg thought to himself that it must all be a dream and that he was still in his warm bed waiting for the alarm to go off, so he could start the morning for real.

A high pitched scream floated to him from a backyard, while he passed a yellow house with white trim, bringing him back to reality

Repressing a shudder, he kept moving.

His house was too far away for him to make it back safely, so he decided to strike out for the police station.

After all, where else would you go if you needed help?

* * *

Rick awoke to the sound of metal clanging on metal. The sound loud enough to override the ringing telephones. Rick had been so tired, he had ignored them.

He looked up from the desk he was sitting at and looked around the station.

It was still totally empty.

No one had come back. How could that be? Surely a few cops would have returned to the station before going home for the night.

Rubbing his face with his hands to try to wake up, he frowned when two paperclips fell from his face onto the desk. Feeling his cheek with his hand, he was amused to find the impressions of the clips in his skin. The clanging started again so he moved around the room, trying to figure out where it was coming from.

Then he heard a low voice calling for help.

"Hello? Is anyone out there? Come on, man, I'm starving down here. Hello!"

Rick moved to the stairs that led down to the cells on the lower level of the police station. With his hand on his weapon, he slowly crept down the stairs. Upon reaching the bottom, he flicked on the light to see one large man sitting in one of the three jail cells.

"Finally, hey, buddy, how 'bout some breakfast? I'm starving," the man said while placing the metal cup he'd been banging against the bars onto the floor of his cell.

Rick moved closer to the cell, but not so close that the guy could grab him.

"Who are you?" Rick asked.

"Who am I? I'm Mary fuckin' Poppins and I flew in yesterday on my umbrella. Who the hell do you think I am? You guys put me in here," the big man quipped.

Rick looked the man over. He was a big guy, at least six-two. He had big hands the size of hams and his hair was cut a little like the King used to cut it.

The man had a southern drawl to his voice that reminded him of Elvis a little, too.

But the more Rick looked at the big man the less he felt threatened. There seemed to be a flicker in his eyes that said he was all bluster.

Rick decided to put his assumption to the test.

"Look, there's nobody upstairs but me. I have no idea where everybody is. Why are you here, what did you do?"

"Me?" The big man asked. "Well, I got caught driving without a license, so the cop towed my Cadillac and brought me here. I tell ya, so help me if my Caddy's scratched."

"So, you don't know about what's going on out there, do you?" Rick asked.

"Out where? What the hell are you talking about, man? Look, I just want some breakfast and another phone call so I can call for bail."

Rick moved closer to the cell. "Look, mister..."

"Just call me Bub, everybody does," he finished.

Rick smiled a little. "Okay, Bub, look, there's some weird shit going down out there. Last night I saw a bunch of crazies kill and eat my backup and the phones have been ringing off the hook with people saying their being attacked. And now no one's come back to the station. At the moment I'm the only one here, and I really don't know what to do, I've been a cop for only three weeks, and I'm not trained for this, and..." Rick would have continued to ramble, the stress catching up to him, when Bub put his hands up for Rick to stop.

"Whoa, buddy, slow down. You're gonna throw a gasket," Bub said, trying to calm the young officer down.

"Now, look, if what you say is true, then what do you say about let me out of here? I can help you. I'm not a real criminal. I just lost my license for too many speeding tickets, that's all."

Rick frowned. "Shit, Bub, I'd like to help you out, but if I did, I'd probably lose my job, sorry. Tell you what though; I'll go get you something from the vending machine. How's that sound?"

Bub stood there for a moment, looking at Rick. Then he shrugged his big shoulders and smiled.

"Shit, kid, beggars can't be choosers. Just do me a favor and don't get me ham out of the machine, I hate ham."

Rick nodded and smiled. "Sure, I'll see what I can do."

Suddenly an explosion rocked the station, sending Rick flying against the cell. If it wasn't for Bub reaching out and catching him, Rick probably would have cracked his skull on the metal bars.

Regaining his balance, Rick looked back up the stairs.

"What the hell was that?" He yelled.

"I don't know, dude, but after you check, don't forget my sandwich," Bub reminded him.

Rick nodded and took off up the stairs, taking them two at a time.

Reaching the top, he moved to the front doors, looking through the now shattered glass.

He was able to see the street clearly, despite the smoke.

As the wind pushed the smoke away, his jaw dropped when he scanned the buildings across the street.

Before there had been a body shop on the opposite side of the police station, now there was nothing but a smoking hole. The stone building that had been between the body shop and the police station was nearly demolished, taking the brunt of the blast.

Despite that, the police station's windows had all been shattered as well as all the glass in the cars on the street.

Rick stepped outside, surveying the damage. The remains of a bus could be seen in the wreckage.

Had the bus plowed into the body shop and set off some flammable chemicals?

There was no way to tell.

Rick kept waiting to hear the sound of sirens from the fire department, but after a full ten minutes had come and gone, he decided they weren't coming.

Walking back inside, he also noticed that all the phones had gone silent.

Looking out the doors again, he saw the telephone lines had been destroyed as well. The long black wires draped across the shattered remains of the cars across the street.

Oh, well, so much for calling for help, Rick thought.

Not having a clue what to do, he locked the front doors. Whatever was going on, he wanted to make sure it stayed outside.

Then he went to the break room vending machine to grab Bub a sandwich. Thinking about not getting ham for the big guy made him smile.

Pumping in five bucks, he picked tuna salad for Bub and a corn beef on rye for himself.

Retrieving the sandwiches, he headed off for the cells. The lights flickered for a moment, causing Rick to pause while he looked up at the lights on the ceiling.

After a moment when he was pretty sure they were going to stay on, he breathed a sigh of relief.

Things may have been bad, but at least he still had power. Smoke from the fires in the shattered buildings across the street blew in through the broken windows of the police station, making Rick wince with the smell.

For a moment, he thought about going over and seeing if any one needed help, but decided against it, after all, he was only one man.

What the hell was he supposed to do?

Stomping down the stairs, he went back to the cells with Bub's breakfast in hand.

*   *   *

Outside the police station, the driver to the bus slowly picked himself up.

He'd been attacked on the first stop of his route, an old lady taking his throat out in one bite.

Later, while still in the driver's seat, the worms had revived him and the ghoul had driven the bus down the street. Not really knowing how to drive now, but some latent memory keeping his foot on the gas, the bus managed to stay in the middle of the road.

At least until it had reached a corner. Not remembering how to turn the large vehicle, the ghoul had plowed into a building, the resulting explosion sending the driver flying through the bus' side window to land on a perfectly manicured lawn across the street, in between some shrubs.

Now it slowly stood on charred legs. Its entire body was blackened from the blast, the grass putting out the rest of the flames when it had landed.

Blackened hands reached out in front of it as it shambled back onto the sidewalk.

Only one red eye still worked; the other dissolving in the heat of the explosion.

It looked up and down the street, trying to find fresh meat.

When none could be seen it shambled onward. It felt no pain now, the only feeling it now knew was hunger.

With a crackling of burnt skin it shuffled away. It would find prey soon; it just had to be patient.

Chapter 12

John stretched in his chair, his eyes never leaving the snowy screen on the little black and white television.

Since he had woken up from an uncomfortable night in his office chair, the news on the television had only gotten worse.

Channel 25 had some scientist on, talking about the current situation the United States now found itself in. He was telling the interviewer that what was happening was not from terrorism like the government first thought.

No, he was saying that for some indecipherable reason the dead were walking.

John had sat up straight in his chair when he'd heard this and had leaned forward to turn the volume up as loud as it would go.

The geeky looking scientist on the screen nodded slightly and the interviewer asked him something else.

"Yes, that's what I said, you heard me correctly," the scientist replied. "The dead appear to be walking. Something, we don't know what yet, seems to be reanimating corpses. Once the corpses return to life, or should I say, non-life, as some of my colleagues have said, the corpses seem to immediately attack any live animal they can get their hands on. They then proceed to feed on them, for what we don't know yet, as nourishment is out of the question. The research is ongoing, you understand."

"Let me get this straight, Dr. Thompson, you're telling me and the viewers that the dead are walking like in some bad 1960's horror movie? That's the most ridiculous thing I've heard this year. And let me tell you, I've heard some crazy shit. Oh my, did you get that, can you bleep that last part out?" The interviewer asked the producer.

The producer pointed angrily to the 'live on air' sign and the interviewer frowned.

"Sorry, folks, I let that one slip, but can you blame me? I mean, come on, Doctor, the dead don't walk, it's impossible."

Dr. Thompson pushed his glasses further up his nose. "Well, my dear sir, whether you want to believe it or not, it is true and they are walking. The only question now is why and how do we stop it."

"Why does the how of it even matter?" The interviewer asked.

"Well, sir, you see, the dead outnumber the living about a million to one. If we don't deduce the cause of this virus and stop it in a matter of weeks, a month at most, the living will be so out-numbered that we could very well find ourselves in a battle for the very survival of mankind."

The interviewer just sat there, with his mouth hanging open.

"That's got to be the biggest bunch of horseshit I've ever heard," the interviewer said as he looked off camera. John figured he was looking at the producer again.

"Yeah, I know what I said, so what?" The interviewer said. "According to this guy, it's the end of the friggin' world."

The interviewer looked at the camera again, sitting up a little taller in his chair.

"All right then, we go live now to Stephanie Wong, who's in New York. Stephanie?"

A pretty Asian woman in her mid-thirties appeared on the screen. Behind her in the background, people were running in panic, and police cars and fire trucks screamed by her, the camera catching it all in panoramic widescreen.

John watched as a running man was tackled by another man, the attacker sinking his teeth into his victim's neck and shoulder; the camera focusing on the carnage.

Stephanie began to speak. "What we have here is total chaos. I'm standing here on..."

She was cut off in mid-sentence when a middle-aged woman in a gray power suit attacked her.

Stephanie went to the sidewalk with a *wumph*, her breath leaving her upon impact with the cold cement. She struggled with her assailant, calling for the camera guy to help her. After a moment, the camera guy came to his senses and left the camera to help Stephanie.

The camera was still catching most of the scene; while Stephanie fought the woman off; the camera guy grabbed her collar from behind and tried to pull her off Stephanie. That's when the crazy woman turned to face the camera guy.

Without hesitation, she sank her teeth into his cheek, ripping a large piece from his face.

With half his cheek gone, the man screamed for God to help him.

John watched the man turn to face the camera. There was a hole in his face where his left cheek used to be, the man's tongue clearly visible from inside his mouth.

John was just glad the set was a black and white television, because he wouldn't have wanted to see that visceral scene in HD.

The woman jumped him again, ignoring his screams for help and proceeded to tear into him with her nails and teeth. Someone's kicking legs knocked over the camera, because in the next second, the picture became sideways.

The camera guy's body was now lying face down on the sidewalk, a growing pool of blood forming under his cheek and neck. As for Stephanie, there was no sign.

Then the screen went black and then came back on with the interviewer's face again.

The man looked how John felt after witnessing what they'd just seen.

The interviewer babbled for a few seconds and then the channel cut to a commercial.

Before John turned the television off, he saw the image of a bouncing cold sore jumping on a woman's face and the name of the medicine at the bottom of the screen.

He leaned back in his chair, thinking about what he'd just seen and heard.

He remembered what had happened last night. The guy he'd hit with his car had clearly not been alive, as hard as that was to believe.

But how can you believe something that's so far fetched, even when you've seen it with your own eyes?

Deep in thought, he stood up from the desk while stretching. It was mid-morning and he'd already decided if he couldn't reach his employers, and no one showed up to relieve him, he'd just say screw it and leave.

But for now he was still working, so with another stretch of tired limbs, he decided to go for a walk and check the building's floors.

*   *   *

The elevator chimed its arrival and he stepped inside.

Pressing the number twelve, he waited as the doors closed and then felt the familiar sensation while the car moved up the shaft.

Thirty seconds later, he stepped out onto the top floor of the office building. Moving to the side window, he looked out across the town of Wakefield.

Through the trees, he could see the very top of another office building. The five year old complex was called Edgewater and John still remembered what had happened there a few years ago.

A disgruntled employee had returned one morning with an assault weapon and had killed six people. The police had eventually arrested him, but it was too late for his once fellow office workers.

John still got a chill whenever he thought about it. If the guy had worked in John's building, it would have been John who was his first victim before the guy went looking for other targets.

After all, in every horror movie made it's always the security guard who bites it first; never fail.

Brushing the dark thoughts away, he changed the direction of his gaze.

Off to his left was a large church situated against a lake, its spires standing majestic against the sky.

The lake's real name was Lake Quannaupawitt, but he'd always called it the Wakefield Lake; like many others who lived near the town, but not in it.

There was a playground next to the church, its swings and monkey bars empty.

That was odd for this time of day. He guessed people were staying inside everywhere. After all it was midmorning and he was still waiting to see someone else who worked in the building arrive.

Next to the church was a small cemetery. The Old Burying Ground, he'd read one day on the internet, when he was bored.

He could see small figures moving around the cemetery, but didn't give it much thought. As he continued to watch, he noticed Church Street had multiple accidents on its two lanes of hardtop. Squinting, he noticed there were many figures lying prone on the ground while others were running around. There were still no police or ambulances, though.

Turning to his right, he looked out across I-95. That was his ticket home and he frowned when he saw the condition of it now.

He couldn't see as much as he would have wanted due to the distance, but he could definitely see a tanker truck lying sideways on the highway.

Smoke rose from some part of it and the traffic was backed up for miles.

Great, he thought, so much for getting home the easy way.

Suddenly, there was a flash of light and the tanker went up like a Roman candle.

A huge fireball rolled across the highway, catching cars and people in the blast.

A second later the echo of the blast reached him. Even through the special soundproof windows of the building, he heard it; and felt it.

A slight tremor seemed to suffuse the building for a moment and then was gone.

John watched the highway burn, small figures moving around in panic.

Looking out across the north side of Wakefield, his heart sank even more.

The city had multiple fires burning on its suburban streets; the smoke rising into the clear blue sky.

He looked down into the parking lot surrounding the office building, his Honda sitting peacefully in its spot by the front door, next to the security pickup truck.

He was supposed to drive around the large lot and make sure there were no kids parking for make out sessions or people parking cars there overnight or for the weekend. With everything that was happening, he'd already decided he'd pass on that part of his job description.

Then he spotted a pedestrian running up the long open driveway that led from the street, the figure's hair blowing in the wind. Behind this lone figure there was a group of people chasing her. Or John assumed it was a woman as the pedestrian's form was petite.

When the figure drew closer, it was clear to John it was a woman. She appeared to be carrying something, but he was too high up to figure out what it could be. With one final look at the town, he ran back to the elevator, punching the call button.

Stepping inside, he pressed the lobby button. With the doors sliding shut, he anxiously waited for the car to reach the lobby; the time it took now seeming painfully long.

With a gentle chime the doors opened and he jumped through them. Grabbing his keys while he ran by the front desk, he ran to the front lobby doors.

By now the woman was only fifteen feet away and as John nervously fiddled with his master keys, the woman ran into the doors, pounding on them.

Through the glass her muffled, terrified voice seeped to John's ears.

"Please help me, they're almost here. Please don't let them get me!" She pleaded.

For a moment John wondered if he'd be able to find the door keys in time, then the correct one fell into his hand.

With practiced experience, he slipped the key into the lock. Pushing the door open, he reached out and grabbed the woman's arm, pulling her inside.

But not before the first man in line chasing her was able to wedge his hand in the gap of the now closing door.

John kept pushing the door closed, his full body weight now leaning against the glass, but the guy wouldn't back off.

With a growl that came from deep in his throat the man tried to push himself forward.

John looked over the man's shoulder and saw he had about ten seconds before the others in the following group were on him, so he made a fast decision.

Letting up on the door, the man fell inside the lobby, caught off balance by the lessening pressure on the glass.

John grabbed the man by his collar and pulled him all the way into the lobby.

Then with the door clear, he slammed it shut, locking the door again.

Not a moment to soon either. No sooner had the lock turned then the others following slammed against the hardened glass.

The first ones in line were crushed flat to the glass panes as the ones behind continued to push.

John only had a second to notice this before he was called back inside by the screams of the woman he'd just saved.

The man was on his feet again and now walking towards the petrified woman.

John moved quickly, getting between the two of them.

"Now, look, buddy, I don't know what's going on here but you need to leave the lady alone," John said, noticing the man's red eyes.

The man just growled, taking a swipe at John.

"Be careful, mister, he's one of them. Don't let him bite you!" She warned, hiding behind John.

A muffled cry came to his ears and he realized the woman was carrying a baby.

"One of them? What the hell are you talking about?" He asked.

"He's one of the crazies, he's infected. If you don't kill him, believe me, he'll kill you," she said.

The whole time John was having his conversation with the frightened woman, the man was trying to get them, but for the moment John was able to fend him off.

"Look, lady, I'm not killing anybody. We just need to talk some sense into him, that's all."

Unfortunately the man didn't agree with John. He lunged at John with raised arms. John tried to fend him off but the man got under his guard.

Half a heartbeat later, John found himself on the cold marble floor of the lobby with the lunatic sitting astride his chest.

John couldn't throw the guy off of him, he was too heavy.

With teeth bared the man tried to bite John's exposed neck. Grunting with the exertion, John was able to keep his teeth away, but the guy was bigger than John and was slowly overpowering him.

Inch by inch, those yellow teeth came closer to the inevitable.

John could already imagine the pain when those teeth sank into his neck, ripping his flesh and veins to shreds. The face was only inches from John's now, the man's fetid breath blowing over John's nose and mouth.

The man's red eyes bore into his, sending a shiver up his back.

John didn't quite know what he was seeing in those eyes, but it wasn't a sane man.

With the man's jaw only a hairs breath away from his neck John grunted, knowing what was coming.

All he could do was pray it would be quick.

Chapter 13

Tommy Garris leaned back in the rear seat of his 1985 Dodge van.

Outside in the streets, the crazy people shambled about, looking for fresh meat.

That was fine with Tommy. He was safe in his van, the crazies not knowing he was there.

Tommy barely paid them any attention.

At the moment, all Tommy's attention was focused on the two-story, vinyl-clad home across the street.

He was parked at the end of Jackson Street.; one of the nicer streets in Wakefield. The street ended in a dead end, the wide circle at the end the perfect place to park his van. The reason he was so focused on the vinyl clad house was because it was on fire.

The fire had started on the small front porch with nothing more than a half gallon of gas and a match.

Tommy should know; he was the one who started it.

It had been so simple. Most of the neighboring homes were empty, the occupants trying to escape the crazies for someplace safer; not realizing they were making it all too easy for him.

The blaze across the street grew higher with the wood of the porch really starting to burn. The front of the house was now catching fire, the flames crawling up to the second floor.

Sitting in the back seat of the van, he couldn't help himself and his right hand slowly crawled inside his pants.

His eyes watched the dancing flames as they swayed in the wind, the oranges and reds an aphrodisiac to his senses.

Ever since he had been a kid, Tommy had always loved fire.

When he was seven he'd been playing with matches under his parent's porch and had accidentally set the wood on fire.

The flames had started slow and then with more of the fifty year old wood to feed it, the fire had consumed the porch and had then covered the entire house.

Two hours later, his family home was burned to the ground.

He'd gone to stay with his Aunt after that; at least until the insurance check had come in to his parents.

His parents had never looked at him the same again, though. As if they too sensed his unnatural attraction to the flame.

He had burned his house down when he was seven and now, years later and more psychiatrists then he could count, he was doing what he had dreamed for the last eleven years.

Reaching a climax, he removed his hand and reached for a tissue.

The house was now fully consumed by flames, the blaze threatening to spill over to the next house.

That would be fine with Tommy. Hell, he'd be happy if the whole town went up in one giant fireball.

His passion appeased for the time being, he started the van and drove down the street.

The crazies tried to reach him, but he just knocked them aside with his van. Leaving the street behind, he turned onto the main road, following it wherever it went.

He would know the next house to burn when he saw it. It would just jump out at him, beckoning him to set it on fire.

The smell of gasoline drifted to his nose. Turning, he looked over the seat to make sure the gas cans were safe. He had four, five gallon cans of gas with him and there was no one to stop him from using them.

Ever since the night before, the police and fire department had been running around like idiots, leaving him free reign with the entire town.

Looking at all the houses as he passed them by, he found himself rubbing his crotch. His arousal was already starting to grow again.

For eleven years he'd been holding back, too scared to light a fire for fear of prosecution. But now he was free to do whatever he wanted.

Turning a corner, he found himself driving up Water Street, the long winding road full of possible targets.

Still he drove.

After all, what was the rush? He had all the time in the world.

And if he had his way, he'd burn it all to the ground in one glorious conflagration of flames and destruction.

Chapter 14

Greg leaned against a graffiti-covered, no parking sign, the police station finally in sight.

It had been a perilous journey on foot across the once quiet town of Wakefield, but he'd finally made it.

Crossing the street warily, he kept his eyes peeled for any more crazies. There had been a few close calls on his way to the police station.

One of which almost cost him his life.

He had been cutting through a manicured backyard when he had come upon a group of crazies.

At first they hadn't noticed him. They were much too busy ripping some poor bastard apart.

There was blood everywhere, the ghouls covered from head to toe. Then one of them had seen Greg and with a moaning sound, had turned and started for him.

Knowing what would happen if he stuck around; he took off at a run down the street he now found himself on.

Keeping ahead of his pursuers, he noticed that most of the houses on this block were brand new duplexes. Lately, they'd been springing up all over the suburbs, north of Boston.

He was slowly pulling away from his pursuers when he saw others in front of him coming straight towards him.

Feeling like a rat in a cage, he stopped running, now standing in the middle of the two groups of crazies. His eyes scanned the area around him, while he frantically tried to decide where to go.

Then his eyes settled on an unfinished duplex situated across the street. Taking off like a sprint runner, he darted for the building, his pursuers close behind.

Stumbling over a two by four, Greg jumped inside the first floor, nothing but heavy plastic on the walls to keep out intruders.

That was good for him, as he was able to get inside, but it was also bad, because the nutcases outside could follow him easily. There was an unfinished wooden staircase to his right and he ran up them, taking the stairs two at a time.

Reaching the second floor, he looked around, frantically searching for a place to hide. There was nowhere to go, the entire floor was nothing but wood framing for the walls and sheets of plastic.

He stopped walking when the sounds of many feet on the bare plywood floor drifted up to him from the first floor.

His heart was beating so fast, he thought it would explode. He swore under his breath when he realized he was in plain view to anybody who came up the stairs, so he decoded to move further into the house.

His foot caught on an extension cord, and a circular saw crashed to the floor.

No sooner had the sound faded then Greg could hear footsteps coming up the stairs after him. Running to the back of the wide open floor, he came up short at the far wall.

He was trapped!

Moaning drifted to him now, the first of his pursuers reaching the top of the stairs.

Wondering how the hell he was going to get away in one piece, his foot kicked something on the floor.

Looking down he saw a battery operated nail gun.

Picking it up, he saw it held a full load. The three inch nails were barbed so they wouldn't wiggle loose over time in the wood.

Setting his jaw, he decided that if he was going down, then he was going to take as many of the bastards with him as he could.

So he started across the floor, the plastic sheets blowing in the wind from the unfinished, open windows. The first figure loomed behind a sheet of plastic and Greg snuck up on him from behind.

Before his quarry knew he was there, he jammed the nail gun into the guy's back, squeezing the trigger three times in quick succession.

He waited for the expected cry of pain from the wounded man, but none came.

Instead the man turned, and in one fluid motion, crashed through the plastic, knocking Greg over to the floor.

They both landed in a puff of sawdust, the man firmly on top of Greg.

Greg panicked and stuck the nail gun in the guy's already mutilated face.

He squeezed the trigger two more times, the nails sinking into flesh and lodging in the man's forehead.

The man didn't even notice as he wrapped his hands around Greg's throat and started squeezing.

Greg felt his consciousness slipping away while he gasped for breath.

With the last of his strength, he raised the nail gun one final time, pressing the muzzle directly over his attacker's left eye.

Then he squeezed the trigger. He kept squeezing repeatedly until the hands loosened on his neck, the man falling to his side to land heavily on the wooden floor with a half dozen, three-inch nails imbedded in its brain.

Greg took deep breaths, filling his lungs with the oxygen they so sorely needed, but he didn't have long to recover. Already more of the crazies were moving around the room to get at him.

Laying there with a dead body next to him, he just realized he'd just killed a man. Whether it was self defense or not, he'd have a lot of explaining to do sooner or later.

Rolling to his feet, he noticed the man he'd perforated with the nail gun had an eye full of the long barbed nails. Some of them were in so deep the man's brain had been punctured.

Brushing the scene aside as irrelevant, figuring the first order of business was to escape, he stood on shaky legs and moved towards the far wall, his pursuers already reaching for him.

The first one tried to grab him and he placed the nail gun against the man's arm. Multiple pulls of the trigger later and the man had an arm that looked like a pincushion. The man didn't act like he felt the pain from the wounds.

Greg was starting to panic. How do you stop an attacker that doesn't feel pain?

His back came up against the back wall and he turned to see there was a window there.

Connected to the window was a long plastic tube about two feet wide, more than large enough to fit a man.

He didn't know where it went, but at the moment he was out of options, so after throwing the nail gun at one of his pursuers, the gun bouncing off a woman's chest, he dived head first into the tube and prayed for the best.

Before he could even scream his head plowed into cardboard boxes.

Covered in dust, he shook his hair and looked around himself. He was in a dumpster at the side of the duplex.

Standing up on the refuse, he climbed up and over, landing on the dirt ground butt first.

Regaining his footing, he looked around and breathed a sigh of relief to see the area around him was empty. At the moment he was the only person there.

Jogging off through the pallets of wood, he smiled. He was one lucky bastard.

Reaching the street, he poked his head around a port-a-potty to make sure the coast was clear.

Satisfied, he took off at a steady jog, his adrenaline still pumping.

The police station wasn't too much farther and hopefully they would know what to do when he arrived there.

Chapter 15

Rick had no idea what he should do.

Standing at the front doors to the police station, he looked out at what was once a quiet street.

Now it looked like a war zone. The fires from the exploding body shop still burned, the flames having more than enough fuel to continue for days if they weren't extinguished.

Rick thought he saw movement in the bushes to his left and was about to investigate when Bub started yelling to him.

Sighing, Rick turned away from the doors. What did that man want now? Rick thought.

Moving down the back stairs, Rick walked out to the cells and Bub.

"What can I do for you, Bub?" Rick asked.

"Well, for starters you could let me out. Look, if what you said is true about what's going on outside, then where the hell am I gonna go?" Bub asked.

Rick thought about that for a moment. Truth be told, he couldn't see any reason why not to let the big man out right now. But he was still concerned about what would happen if one of his superiors showed up.

"I'll tell you what, Bub. I'll make a deal with you. If none of my boss' shows up by tonight then I'll let you out, deal?"

Bub barely hesitated. "Deal," he said, holding his hand out through the bars for Rick to shake.

Rick stared at the meaty paw and then took it, both men shaking twice before letting go.

Rick was about to ask Bub something else when he heard a banging coming from upstairs.

"You hear that? Someone's at your front door," Bub said.

"Yeah, I can hear, too, you know. I'll be right back," Rick said, moving up the stairs.

"Don't worry, I'll be here," Bub replied to Rick's back before the man had disappeared from view.

With nothing else to do, Bub lay down on his small bed and closed his eyes, wishing to God he had a television to pass the time.

*   *   *

The banging grew louder the closer Rick got to the first level. Moving through the desks, he spotted a man standing at the front door.

The man spotted Rick and called to him.

"Officer, why the hell is this door locked? Let me in. There's some of those crazy bastards following right behind me!" Greg yelled, frantically looking over his shoulder.

With his hand on his weapon Rick moved to the door.

"Who are you, what do you want?" Rick asked softly.

"What!" Greg yelled. "This is a fucking police station isn't it? For the love of God open the damn doors!" He screamed, shaking the doors with his hands.

Rick's hands reached for the lock and no sooner was the door unlocked, than Greg plowed into the station, nearly knocking Rick to the floor.

Behind him Rick saw something blackened and burned shambling up the police station steps.

"What the fuck is that?" He gasped.

The figure that stood on the steps resembled a human being in form only. Where skin used to be there was nothing but blackened, brittle flesh. Wherever the flesh was peeling, there were red rivulets of blood dripping out of the wounds.

The red, baleful eyes had sunk back into the face and the hair was nonexistent.

The smell of burnt bacon drifted to Rick's nose, strong enough to make him gag.

He stood very still, not comprehending what he was seeing, his mind refusing to believe the figure in front of him was possible.

It couldn't exist.

But yet it did.

The mouth opened, burnt vocal cords trying to speak, but nothing came out but a dry, rasping groan.

The figure had made it nearly to the top by now, only a few feet from Rick. Still, he stood there, the shock of the burnt zombie paralyzing him.

The burnt corpse reached out, ready to grab Rick.

When Greg's arm shot past Rick and wires shot into the ghoul's charred chest.

The zombie began to twitch, the smell of burnt meat growing worse. Then the walking corpse fell back down the steps, rolling the last few as it came to rest on the sidewalk, the wires becoming entangled in its limbs.

Rick had come to, as well. He looked askance to see Greg standing next to him with a police issue taser in his hand.

Finished with the weapon, Greg tossed it to the concrete stairs.

"Take that, you bastard," he said, admiring his handiwork.

Then he slapped Rick on the back.

"Hey, thanks, I didn't think I was gonna make it there for a second," Greg said.

"Are you coming back inside?" Greg finished.

Rick nodded and stepped into the police station, securing the door again. Then he looked at Greg.

"That was quick thinking. Where'd you find that taser?" Rick asked.

"It was on one of the back desks. Good thing, too, huh?" Greg replied.

Bub's voice floated from down below.

"Hey, Rick, what's going on up there?" The big man called.

"Who's that?" Greg asked.

"I've got a prisoner in one of the cells. His name's Bub. But don't worry, he's harmless," Rick said, moving to the break room.

Greg followed, looking around the station.

"So, uh, where the hell is everyone?" Greg asked.

Rick shrugged. "Couldn't tell you. Out there fighting the bad guys, I guess."

"You mean the crazies?" Greg asked.

"The what? What are you talking about?" Rick inquired.

"The crazy people. Look, all I know is I got up for work today and found the whole damn town had gone crazy. There's people out there attacking and eating other people. Come on, man, you must know about it. You're a cop, for Christ's sake."

Rick thought back to the night before and all the weird phone calls he'd answered before the lines went down.

"Yeah, I guess I know about it. What do you think happened? Terrorists maybe, you know, like biological warfare or something."

Greg shook his head. "Look, man, I don't know nothin' about any shit like that. I work in an office supply store, for God's sake. That's why I ran here. I didn't know where else to go. Have you called for help? When's the National Guard or the State Police showing up?"

"Hell, man, I wish I knew. The phones are out. I figured I'd just stay here until help arrives," Rick said.

Greg nodded. "Yeah, I guess, what else is there to do? Hey, listen, I've been running all morning, do you have any place where I can wash up and get something to drink?"

Rick pointed to a door by the break room. "Right there, it's a bath-room."

Greg smiled. "Thanks, I'll be right out."

Rick turned to go down stairs to see Bub. "Yeah, fine, just come downstairs when you're done, okay?"

With a wave of assent, Greg disappeared into the bathroom.

Rick frowned slightly. Was it possible only one lone civilian out of the thousands living in the town had managed to get to the police station?

Where the hell was everybody?

Bub called up to him and he lost his train of thought.

"All right, all right, I'm comin'," Rick said while moving down the stairs.

*   *   *

In the dark streets of Wakefield, Massachusetts, and across the United States, the spreading fires raged and the walking dead continued adding to their numbers.

The collapse of civilization was happening very smoothly, actually.

No one would believe what was happening could possibly be real, assuming it was terrorists or biological warfare, much like Rick had assumed.

Most people were in total denial, refusing to believe what the news broadcasts were saying.

That the dead were somehow walking.

In less than twenty-four hours, the number of undead had risen to thousands, their army steadily growing.

The only real question would be; would people accept the unacceptable before it was too late?

Chapter 16

Kim slowed the SUV at the next intersection. She'd been driving for two hours, not sure exactly where she was supposed to go or what she should do.

The streets were nothing but chaos. Everywhere she looked, there were people running around attacking other people.

Even the animals were infected. About an hour ago she'd been driving down by the high school when she had to stop short in the road.

Sitting in the middle of the street were four large dogs. Kim sat still, watching them, wondering what they intended to do. For the moment, she felt safe behind the glass and steel of the vehicle, the dogs just watching her.

Then one of them had walked towards her and had jumped onto the hood of her vehicle.

She sounded the horn, but the animal wasn't even phased.

It leaned forward, its tongue hanging out and had put its muzzle not more than an inch from the windshield.

This close, Kim could see its red eyes clearly as they stared at her through the glass.

While Kim watched the animal, she started to notice its fur was rippling; almost as if there was something crawling underneath its skin.

Then through a wound the dog had on its shoulder Kim saw tiny maggots crawl out and fall to the hood of her SUV, where they twitched in the morning sun.

Kim was beyond grossed out and had decided she'd seen enough. Revving the engine, she moved the vehicle forward just enough to let the dog know he had to leave or risk falling off the hood.

The dog was oblivious, its eyes continuing to stare at Kim.

That was when she floored the pedal, the dog slipping on the hood and falling hard onto the metal. The inertia of the SUV had the dog hitting the windshield, but then Kim hit the brakes, sending the dog flying off the hood to land in the street.

The dog stood up wobbling, one of its legs clearly broken from the fall.

Kim cut the wheel and swerved around it, the other animals moving out of the way as she sped past.

She checked her rearview mirror once to see if they were chasing her and was relieved to see they were still sitting in the street.

She slowed the SUV; now comfortable with the distance she had from the animals and watched them in her rearview for a few more seconds.

Then as one the animals shot off across the street to be lost in the backyard of a one family home.

Kim stayed and watched the empty road for another second and then began driving again. What the hell had she just seen, and how did it relate to what was going on around her?

Turning another corner she saw a small group of people walking on the sidewalk.

Heading for them, she rolled down her window to ask them if they knew what was going on in town.

Pulling up next to them, she paused at the condition of the group.

The woman closest to Kim had her chest ripped open, her clothes covered in blood and gore.

The man next to the woman had one arm missing and his throat had been ripped from left to right, giving him the illusion of a second, larger mouth below his real one.

There was a child in the middle of the group, no more than nine or ten years old.

Kim saw the boy was gnawing on a severed arm, and when her eyes noticed the man who was missing his appendage, Kim realized that the cloth on the man and the severed arm were a perfect match.

Kim let out a scream that should have shattered the glass in her vehicle.

Pressing the gas pedal, she shot down the street, leaving the ragtag group of ghouls behind.

What the hell was going on? Those people should be dead, not going for a stroll.

Her eye caught the sign for the Wakefield Police Station and she thought that would be a good place to go, considering what was happening.

She should be able to get help there.

Getting herself back under control, she turned off the main road she was on and headed deeper into town. The police station was close and once she got there, she hoped she'd be safe.

Kim breathed a sigh of relief, the police station just around the corner.

But due to her panic she was driving a little too fast and as she came around the corner, she found five ghouls in front of her.

Instinct took over and she swerved the vehicle hard to the right, trying to avoid running over anyone.

The SUV jumped the curb and Kim found herself driving on the sidewalk.

With cars parked in the street and houses on her right, she had no where to go but straight ahead.

With her heart in her throat she continued moving forward, mailboxes breaking off and bouncing off the hood and grille until she saw a car parked half in the driveway and half on the sidewalk.

There was nowhere for her to go, so she slammed on the brakes, the front of the SUV hitting the parked car, the front bumper pushing in the passenger side door.

The impact was enough to set off the air bag in the steering wheel, the force of the inflating bag hitting her square in the face, knocking her unconscious.

Kim lay oblivious, while the walking corpses surrounded her vehicle.

The ghouls tried to open the doors, but they had locked automatically when the car was placed in drive.

The walking dead started to bang on the glass and doors of the SUV, frustrated that their meal was so close, yet unattainable.

Inside the vehicle, Kim was coming to, not quite comprehending what had happened.

With bleary eyes, she looked around her and her breath lodged in her throat.

The SUV was surrounded by at least seven people, all with strange wounds that should have had them running for the nearest hospital. Instead they were trying to reach her; their red eyes seemed to bore into her as she sat trapped like an animal.

Remembering what her mother had done to the paperboy, she knew it wouldn't be pleasant if they caught her.

Looking through the arms and torsos of the ghouls, she realized she was no more than five houses away from the police station.

The houses in front of her were shattered buildings, as if they had been caught in a blast of some kind. Small fires burned in the wreckage and debris filled the street.

A small part of her wondered what had happened until a ghoul banged on the glass, its face sliding across the smooth surface, leaving behind a trail of blood and yellow pus.

She screamed for help, but soon realized there was no one to hear her or help her.

The panic began to take over, gnawing at her insides like a hundred rats.

Laying on the horn, she kept it pressed, praying someone would hear it and come to her aid. The ghouls continued beating on the SUV. One of them picked up a fist sized rock and started to bang on the windshield.

Small cracks started to appear and began to spider web across the glass. The ghoul was uncoordinated and accidentally crushed some if its fingers between the rock and the glass. The glass became covered in blood, the viscous fluid starting to fill the cracks, slowly following the contour of the windshield.

She screamed again, the panic feeling like it was taking on a life of its own and soon she would have no choice but to let it take over.

Deep down she knew if that happened, then she would be dead in minutes. The moment she attempted to flee the vehicle the zombies would chase her down and kill her.

With the horn blaring, the ghouls pounding on the SUV, and Kim screaming for help, she felt her sanity slowly slipping away.

That's when the passenger side window exploded inward, another zombie with a rock following close behind.

Kim turned to see its face was half missing, the torn flesh still showing the teeth marks where it was ripped off. Maggots squirmed in the flesh, dropping to the leather seats of the SUV while the living corpse climbed through the broken window.

Kim saw all this in slow motion, like someone had pressed the slow, scan button on the movie that was her life.

While the ghoul crawled onto the passenger seat; its bloody hands reaching for her, she felt the little bit of sanity she was holding onto vanish like candle smoke in a windstorm.

The moment the ghoul's hand grabbed her, she started screaming and this time she didn't think she would be stopping until the last breath was taken from her dead body.

Chapter 17

John could feel the breath of his attacker on his neck and the stench made him gag. Just before the ghoul would have ripped his throat out with its teeth, John heard a large crack fill the lobby.

The man on top of him stopped moving and began to spasm. Then there was another crack and John felt a wetness on his cheek, as the man went slack. Throwing his attacker off him with a heave, John was relieved to see the woman he'd saved standing next to him with a heavy glass paperweight taken from the front desk.

Her other hand was still holding the baby protectively.

"Wow, I don't know how to thank you," John said, clumsily coming to a standing position.

She just smiled while she looked at him and then the front glass doors, where the other ghouls still banged on the glass.

John saw the direction of her eyes and followed them with his own, seeing the ghouls banging on the glass.

"Don't worry; they're not getting in here. Those doors are at least an inch thick. That stuff's harder than it looks," he said, trying to calm her.

She nodded and moved closer to him, her eyes never leaving the body on the floor. John looked as well, noticing the gaping fracture in the dead body's skull.

Bits of gray matter could be seen peeking out of the wound.

"Shit, you really clobbered that guy," John said, rubbing his throat.

"I'm sorry, I didn't mean to, but I didn't know what to do. Is he dead?" She said, tears beginning to well up in her eyes.

The baby squawked in her arms, and she glanced down, whispering cooing noises to quiet him.

John watched her and then said: "With a skull fracture like that, oh, yeah, he's dead, but that's fine with me. Better him than me." Then he decided to change the subject to something less gruesome. "What's the little guy's name?" He asked with his most sincere smile.

"This is Vincent. He's named after my husband's father," she said, the tears still there, ready to come out at a moments notice. "And I'm Lisa."

John nodded. "Hi, Lisa, I'm John. So, Lisa, where's your husband? With all the crazy shit going on out there, shouldn't he be with you?"

That question started her tears, her cheeks quickly becoming wet.

Through sobs of tears, she told her story to John.

"He's dead. Some of those crazy people got him. But that wasn't the worst part. The worst part was when he came back from the dead and tried to kill me and Vincent."

"What are you saying? That he was some kind of zombie or something, that died and then came back to life? I'm sorry Lisa, that's a little far fetched, I mean they've been saying similar stuff on the television, but it's got to be some kind of a hoax," John said.

While he talked, he was moving the dead body over to the glass doors; at least until he figured out what to do with him.

He assumed the police would be involved, although with the phone lines tied up he didn't know when that would happen.

Dropping the body in the entry, he paused to look at the group of people on the other side of the glass doors.

Their red eyes seemed to glare at him and John knew that if they got into the lobby they would tear him limb from bloody limb.

Repressing a shudder, he moved back to Lisa, who had sat down in the chair at his desk.

John leaned his butt against the desk and smiled at her. After staring at the dead eyes of the other people outside, maybe her story wasn't that crazy.

"Okay, you know what, maybe I'm wrong. Why don't you start over," John said.

Lisa looked up at him, her eyes full of emotion; seeing he was sincere, she nodded. "All right, I'll try."

"This morning was like any other morning in my house. My husband Mickey was getting ready for work and I was in the kitchen making breakfast.

I was feeding Vincent his formula when I heard a crash outside on the front lawn.

I called to Mickey, and told him what had happened. He threw on some clothes and before I could tell him more, he was running outside with a baseball bat.

You see, we've had some trouble with vandalism lately, you know, spiked tires and the car getting keyed.

So Mickey runs outside while I watch from the front window. There are three guys on our lawn. Mickey tells them to get lost, but they just stare at him. So Mickey moves closer, waving his bat at them and telling them if they don't leave then he's going to call the police.

But instead of leaving they attack Mickey. I'd heard what they said on the news about crazy people, but I didn't think it was happening here in our own town.

While I watched, the three of them attacked my husband. Mickey put up a good fight, caving one of the attacker's head in with the bat, but the other two didn't even slow down. In a moment they were pushing him to the grass and while I watched helpless the two men started to tear my husband apart.

I left the window for a second; going to the phone to try and call for help, but there was no answer at 911. Just a stupid recording saying they were overloaded and to stay on the line.

I swear to you, John, if I had a gun I would have gotten it and used it, but this is Massachusetts and a gun license is hard to get; unless you know somebody.

So anyway, by the time I returned to the window my husband wasn't moving anymore and there were two men leaning over him.

And John... they were eating him.

I saw one of the men rip my husband's chest open with his bare hands and plunge his bloody hands into Mickey's body.

That was when I screamed. I ran to the door and made sure it was locked, and then I ran and got my baby.

The two of us then went into the corner of the living room and prayed the men would leave when they were through with my husband.

About fifteen minutes later though, it got weirder.

I decided to peek through the window just to see if they were gone and I couldn't believe it, but my Mickey was standing up. The other two men seemed to ignore him now and they stumbled away to God knows where. I ran to the door and opened it, calling to Mickey.

I figured maybe his wounds weren't as bad as I'd first thought and if we could get to a hospital quick, he'd be okay.

Mickey turned to see me standing in the doorway when I called and he began walking towards me.

It was when he was only a few feet away and he was climbing up the couple of steps on the porch that I realized he wasn't my Mickey anymore.

Mickey has the bluest eyes I have ever seen. In fact, that was one of the reasons I fell in love with him, but when he was close enough for me to see his face in the morning sun; I saw his eyes were now a deep red color.

And when he was right on top of me I saw his chest wound was horrible. In fact I couldn't imagine how he could be alive with the severity of his wound.

Then he lunged at me. I panicked and tried to slam the door shut, but he was too strong and he forced his way in. Before I could run, my hair was in his fist and he was pulling me towards him.

My baby was in my left hand and he started to cry. I tried to push Mickey away, but he overpowered me. As my baby cried and my hair felt like it was being pulled from its roots, I scrambled for a way to escape.

Before his teeth found me, I noticed the umbrella hanging on the coat rack.

You know it's kind of funny really, I always used to tell Mickey to put the wet umbrellas in the back hall to dry, but he never listened to me, no, he'd just hang it on the coat rack and let the water drip on the carpet. I used to get so mad at him for it, one of my pet peeves I guess.

Sorry, I got off track, John. Nerves, I guess.

Now, when I saw that umbrella, I thought it was my only hope to escape alive with my baby.

I mean, there I was, with my hair in his hands and my other searching for something as a weapon and then I see the umbrella. I reach for it with my free hand and grab it, pulling the coat rack over at the same time.

With the umbrella in my hand, I twisted in Mickey's grip, feeling my hair ripping from my scalp."

She automatically reached up to rub the top of her head, remembering the pain she'd felt.

"Then, God help me. I rammed it into Mickey's right eye. The eye exploded as the umbrella went in and I could feel my stomach getting ready to expel my breakfast.

But then, Mickey's hand let me go and he fell to the steps like he'd been shot.

I panicked then, not knowing what to do, so I ran to the kitchen and grabbed the car keys from the wall. Then with my baby and nothing else, I ran to the side of the house where our car was and I jumped in and drove away.

When I first left the driveway, I didn't really know where to go, and then I decided I'd go to my mother's house in Melrose.

Being that it was the next town over, I didn't think that would be so hard. Boy was I wrong. I hadn't even made it more than a mile when I came upon a car crash.

The whole street was blocked and there was no way around it.

It was then as I tried to turn the car around that I saw them.

It was more of those crazy people; like the ones that had killed my Mickey.

When they saw me in the car they ran over to me and started to bang on the glass and the hood.

I was petrified and was worried what would happen to my baby if they got in, so I floored the gas pedal and ran two of them over.

My God, John, I'm pretty sure I killed them.

Then I backed up and drove the other way.

I thought I'd head for I-95 and then cut over to Route 1, that way I could get to Melrose the long way, but I never got a chance.

After no more than a half mile some idiot plowed into me at an intersection.

I had the green but the other guy didn't seem to care.

Luckily, me and the baby were fine and when I looked up into the other car I saw a woman on top of a man.

And John, she had his ear in her mouth. Then she swallowed it and went in for more. The man was screaming for a few seconds and then it became eerily quiet.

I tried to start the car again, but it wouldn't crank over. Then I saw more of those people coming down the street and I got out of the car and grabbed Vincent. Then I ran for my life and was running all morning until I saw your driveway, and the rest you know," Lisa said, finishing her story.

John had to close his mouth, when he realized it had fallen open for the third time since her story had started.

"Wow, I don't know how to respond to that. All that really happened?"

Lisa looked at him with daggers in her eyes.

"Whoa, okay, calm down, I'm sorry, of course it happened. Uh...wow," he said again. "I'm so sorry you had to go through that... uh wow."

"Will you stop saying wow?" Lisa yelled at him.

"All right, okay, gees, sorry. Well, listen, you're safe now, so why don't you go wash up and stuff. The bathroom's over there," John said, pointing to a door at the end of the lobby.

She nodded and then stood up and walked off to the bathroom, baby Vincent making typical baby noises while she left.

Once she was gone, John sat in the vacated chair. Frowning, he looked out the lobby doors at the people foaming at the mouth to get in and kill them. Then he remembered what he'd seen on the twelfth floor.

Maybe they were better off where they were, instead of trying to leave like he'd first thought. Maybe they were safer here.

Watching the doors jiggle in their frames from the weight of the bodies pushing on them, he still couldn't help wondering if this would be their haven or their tomb.

Chapter 18

Tommy pulled up to a one-family ranch house on Brook Street.

He'd been driving around for hours, waiting for the right house to speak to him. And then he'd heard it.

He hadn't planned to go down this particular street, but a pile up on the main road had left him no choice. So he had detoured around the accident.

As he drove by the two car pile up, he slowed down enough to check it out.

Like most people, he was trying to see if there was any gore to be seen, and he wasn't disappointed.

A Toyota and a minivan had collided and the Toyota had lost. The Toyota's windshield had a gaping, shattered hole in it. In that hole was the now very dead driver of the small car. Tommy drove by and noticed the man's eyes were still open in death, the vacant orbs staring at nothing.

A small chill went up Tommy's back, causing the hair on his neck to tickle.

He had never really seen a sight like the one in front of him in all its visceral realness and found himself turning away.

The driver of the minivan was nowhere to be found. Turning up the side street to see if he could somehow circle around the obstruction, he had slammed on the brakes of his battered Dodge when the house spoke to him.

It wasn't like the house actually talked to him in a conventional sense, but more like soft whispers that came from deep in his subconscious.

So now he sat in front of the house, getting ready to burn it to the ground.

Before he stepped out of the Dodge, he double-checked to make sure the coast was clear; that there were no crazies about.

When he was satisfied with his surroundings, he stepped out and went to the driver's side sliding door.

Opening it, he pulled out one of the cans of gas and walked up to the front of the house, looking so relaxed he could have been mistaken for someone selling newspaper subscriptions.

He didn't know if the house was empty or occupied, but frankly, he didn't care. All he knew was that this particular house needed to burn.

He began pouring the flammable liquid on the front stairs, but then decided to get a little more adventurous. Moving to the side of the house, he started to cover the vintage wood shingles with more of the gas.

When he was finished, he moved to the other side of the house and coated it with the rest of his depleting can.

When the can was empty, he tossed it into the bushes of the neighboring house. He wasn't worried about anyone finding it, as the city seemed to have its own problems at the moment.

He reached into his pocket and pulled out a book of matches.

Only four matches remained.

When he was bored, he would light them and watch the flames, then he'd let the match burn down to his fingers. He would always try to see how long he could hold it until the match either went out or the pain got too much for him.

Separating one of the last few matches from the book, he lit it on the back.

It sputtered to life, giving his insides a tingle.

But then a brisk wind blew it out before he could toss it onto the house's front porch. His mouth went into a frown, much like when a seven year old is told no cookies before dinner.

After double checking his surroundings, he tried another match; with the same results.

Inside he wanted to scream, he now had only two matches left and the cigarette lighter in the Dodge had stopped working years ago.

He was so close and yet so far.

This time he turned away from the wind, hoping his body would do the job of shielding the fragile flame.

With his breath in his throat, he lit the second to last match. The small head sprung to life, and with the utmost care, he stepped close to the house and dropped the match. His luck held and the porch burst into orange and red flames, the porch burning as only an old house can.

Soon the sides had caught as well and the house was a raging inferno. Tommy stood as close as he could, basking in the light and heat.

A burning ember drifted on the wind and seemed to kiss his cheek. The small sting was enough to get him going and he had to run to the van and immediately pull down his pants.

While the house went up in flames, Tommy sat in his van, masturbating. He tried to hold out for as long as he could but the excitement was too much and he popped off.

Laying in his backseat in total satisfaction, he watched the flames grow higher.

As time went by the wind took the burning embers and sent them to the neighboring house. When enough embers had coated it, the new house started to smoke; the original wood shingles the perfect catalyst for the thriving fire.

Tommy watched the second house begin to burn, his excitement growing again.

This was better than he could have hoped.

Then a door to one of the neighboring houses was thrown open and a man came running out with a rifle in his hand.

The man took one look at Tommy's van and raised the weapon.

Tommy knew when it was time to leave, so hopping into the driver's seat; he started the engine and took off down the street.

Behind him the man raised his rifle and in the next second, one of the rear windows of the van's backdoors exploded.

Tommy swerved the van and ducked down as low as he could go. Then he was at the end of the street and turned the corner, in his haste to escape, almost flipping the Dodge onto its side.

Checking his rearview mirror and realizing he was safe, he slowed the van to a more moderate speed.

His adrenaline was pumping and he had never felt as alive as he did right now.

Continuing up the street, he relaxed a little, enjoying the rush.

Behind him the town of Wakefield started to burn, one house at a time.

Chapter 19

Greg had just finished in the washroom and was about to go downstairs with Rick and his hapless prisoner, Bub, when he heard the thumping sound of metal hitting metal coming from outside on the street. He ran to the front doors already knowing what he'd see; a car crash.

Halfway down the block on the other side of the street was a red SUV.

It had collided with another parked car on the sidewalk and was slowly being surrounded by people.

From Greg's personal experience, he knew the people weren't going to the driver's aid.

A few of the men and women seemed to shamble or stumble across the worn concrete, then to actually walk. And even from Greg's vantage point he could see some of them had grave wounds covering their bodies.

Turning from the door, he dashed down the stairs to the cells below, almost slipping in his haste and tumbling head first down the last six steps.

Regaining his footing, he barreled into the room, where he saw Rick standing in front of a cell where a big hulking man was incarcerated.

"Officer," he said, out of breath from his brief sprint. "There's been a car accident down the street. I didn't see whose in there, but if we don't help them soon, those crazy bastards are gonna get them."

Rick stood still for a moment, unable to decide on a course of action, when Bub slapped him on the back.

"Come on, Rick, let me out and I'll help you. I already gave you my word I won't run away. What else do you want from me? Besides, you need all the help you can get," Bub said, trying to sound convincing.

Rick mulled it over. "Well, I don't know. I told you before what would happen if one of my superiors comes back and finds out I let you out."

Greg watched them go back and forth and then interjected himself into the conversation.

"Shit, Officer, have you been outside lately? If someone was coming back here then they'd be here already. Listen, man, you're on your own, and frankly I'd like this guy watching my back," Greg said, pointing to Bub.

"Hey, thanks, man," Bub said to Greg.

Greg smiled back. "Don't mention it. So what's it gonna be Rick? I'd say we have seconds to decide before it won't matter anymore, 'cause the crazies will have grabbed and probably eaten the people in that car."

Rick's shoulders slumped just a little as he gave into the two men's coercion. "Fine, all right, you win, I'll let Bub out and he can help us." Then he went to the wall and hit the release for the jail cell. With an electronic click the cell popped open and Bub exited with a big smile on his face.

"Hot damn, paroled at last."

"Well, save the celebration for later 'cause I need those muscles now," Greg said, turning and running up the stairs.

Rick and Bub followed and soon were at the front doors. Rick surveyed the situation and then held up his finger in a hold that thought gesture. Then the young man disappeared into the back room of the station to reappear two minutes later carrying an assortment of weapons.

"I raided the armory. I figured we're gonna need these," Rick said, placing a few weapons on the nearest desk.

Bub moved to see what the policeman had acquired and blew a soft whistle when he had a better look.

"This is great, man, can I have one?" Bub asked, excited.

With the utmost seriousness, Rick nodded yes. "From now on you two are deputies of the Wakefield Police Department. We'll sort out the fine print later," Rick stated.

"Here, Bub why don't you take this," Rick said, handing the big man a pump action shotgun.

"I assume you know how to use this?" Rick asked.

"Shit, man, is the Pope Catholic?" Bub said. Checking for rounds and upon discovering it was empty, he reached to the box of shells that Rick had brought him and started to load the weapon.

"What about me?" Greg asked.

"Well, I don't know; have you ever fired a gun before?" Rick inquired.

"Uh, actually no I haven't," Greg said, a little ashamed.

"That's okay, why don't you take this stun gun and nightstick and let the rest of us take care of the artillery."

Greg nodded, a little embarrassed. He wanted a gun like the other men, but he knew he'd probably end up shooting his foot off, so he reluctantly agreed. Outside in the street, a horn had started blaring, and the distinct sounds of screaming filled the air.

With his pistol drawn, Rick checked to make sure he had a full clip and then looked at the other two men.

"Looks like our time is up, if we're gonna help, then it's now or never."

"Then let's go man, my trigger finger's itchy," Bub exclaimed, pumping the shotgun.

Rick looked at Greg and the man nodded.

"All right then, let's go, follow me," Rick told them while unlocking the front door and charging into the afternoon sun; with the other two men close behind.

*　　*　　*

Kim was fighting a losing battle against the ghoul who had crawled in through her broken passenger window.

Through sheer desperation she was holding the crazy man off and knew it was almost over.

Then the front windshield sprouted a hole and half the ghoul's head blew apart, spraying her with blood and bits of skull.

For a moment she stopped moving and just stared at the grisly scene in front of her, the shock of it numbing her. The head had slumped into her lap and she could clearly see small worms wriggling around in what was left of the torn and ripped brain.

Gunfire could be heard getting closer to her, but she was oblivious as the shock and terror she'd experienced for the past day finally hit her head-on and she started screaming. She screamed until she started to feel light headed and then without realizing it, she passed out, her head slumping to the glass of the driver's door.

*   *   *

Now outside, the three men moved closer to the SUV. There were about eight people surrounding the trapped vehicle and they weren't very happy about being interrupted.

This was the first time that Bub had a taste of what had been happening since the night before, and he watched the horribly wounded people turn and begin moving towards him. He just stared and uttered a simple: "Holy shit." As if that said it all.

Greg heard him and thought that about summed it up nicely, but before he could say anything witty in reply, a zombie turned and decided he'd be good for a midday snack.

He looked to see where Rick and Bub were, but at the moment he found himself on his own.

The zombie lunged at him and he backed up a step, trying to keep clear of the zombies clutches, but he quickly realized if he wanted to get out of this in one piece, then he was going to have to go on the attack.

So the next time the ghoul reached for him, he brought the nightstick down on bloody fingers. The soft sound of tiny bones breaking drifted to his ears as the zombies hand was shattered under the blow, but Greg noticed the crazy guy didn't seem to mind.

On the next lunge from the ghoul, Greg darted in and jammed the taser against its forehead, and then before he could change his mind, he pressed the button and activated it.

Hundreds of volts of electricity flooded into the ghoul's brain, literally cooking it. With steam seeming to come out of its ears it collapsed onto the street, vanquished.

The smell of cooking meat floated to Greg's nose and he found himself vomiting in the middle of the street. Then with his stomach finished expelling what was left, he backed away from the prone body.

With the nightstick held up in front of himself for protection, he waited for his two companions to finish off the others.

*   *   *

After firing off the shot that went through the windshield, Rick moved closer.

"Look, Bub, I've seen what these crazy bastards can do so don't give them a chance to get close. If they make any threatening move towards you, then you have my permission to take them out."

"Fuckin A," was all Bub said in return.

Bub watched the people from the car move towards him and he couldn't believe his eyes. It was like some parody of a bad horror movie. The men and women in front of him should not be walking around. One man had half his stomach ripped out and there was a woman with more than a third of her throat missing.

Then a man started towards him and he didn't look like he wanted to chat.

Bub stood and waited. Like his father had always told him when they would go hunting together, let the prey come to you. And that's what he did. When the shambling man was only a few feet away, Bub warned him off.

"Look, partner, I don't want to hurt you, but if you don't stop moving then I'm gonna blow a hole in you big enough for my dick to fit. So stop moving."

The man didn't even slow down. Bub backed up a little, not wanting to shoot, but soon realized it was either that or fight the guy hand to hand. Bub knew he could kick the guy's ass, but frankly, after looking at the guy's creepy red eyes and bloody teeth, he didn't want to get that close to him.

So leveling the shotgun, he aimed at the guy's arm.

"Last warning, buddy," Bub said. The man continued forward with an evil gleam in his crimson eyes.

Bub shrugged, he'd done his best to give the guy a chance, now it was on him to keep his promise.

Aiming for the guys left arm, Bub squeezed the trigger of the shotgun. In an instant the man's arm was severed at the elbow, the loose limb falling to the side from the blast.

The man barely noticed.

"What the fuck is this shit?" Bub whispered.

The man moved closer, and in a moment would be in arms reach, so Bub brought the shotgun even with the guy's chest and fired again.

Half the guy's right side exploded in a spray of blood and gore. Internal organs slipped free of their places of residence and fell to the street.

Bub was a hard man, who'd seen hard things in his life, but even he could feel his breakfast rising. Despite two fatal gunshot wounds the man continued forward.

In shock from the bloody, impossible sight in front of him, Bub just stood perfectly still until the ghoul was within arms reach. With its remaining hand, it reached out to grab Bub and that was when the big man snapped out of it.

Pushing the ghoul away from him, he brought up the shotgun and shot the zombie in the head at point blank range. The skull disintegrated instantly, blood spray hitting Bub in the face and chest, covering the street around both killer and victim.

Bub breathed a silent sigh of relief when the now headless body fell to the ground to remain still.

"Okay then, it looks like it's the goddamn head that does the job," he said while looking for another target.

Spotting an old woman who had to be in her late eighties or early nineties, he hesitated. Jesus, he thought, she looks just like my grandmother.

But then Grandma turned his way and hissed at him and with her red eyes creased to slits, she ran at him.

Bub panicked, not used to old ladies attacking him so he pushed her away.

In his panic, he forgot his own strength and sent the old woman to the ground hard, where she promptly broke a hip.

A large piece of bone stood out at an odd angle from her beige slacks, the prone woman now starting to crawl towards Bub.

He took one look at the old lady and muttered: "Oh, man, now that ain't right."

The frail, little old lady continued trying to reach him, but Bub decided she was harmless and stepped over her to find more imposing threats to him and his new found friends.

*   *   *

Rick continued firing his .45 until the clip ran dry. When he was empty, the rest of the ghouls lay dead at his feet. Like Bub, he had fired into their bodies and nothing had happened, then he had shot one in the head, by accident really, and it had fallen to the ground to finally remain still. After that, he'd placed only head shots into the unruly crowd.

The motto he'd had drilled into him from the academy kept floating into his head. To Protect and to Serve, he'd been taught. Except now, he was blowing the heads off the public he had taken an oath to protect.

He pushed those thoughts away for another time. Remembering what had happened to his fellow officers at the mortuary, he knew he was doing what had to be done if he wanted to save the driver of the SUV and himself.

With all the ghouls down, he moved to the driver's door of the crashed vehicle, with Bub and Greg watching his back.

"You guys okay?" Rick asked, pulling open the door.

"Yeah, it's cool, can't say I found that enjoyable, though," Bub said.

Greg looked at the two of them.

"All I know is that I'm not doing that again without a gun," Greg said, his head constantly moving, as if he expected a ghoul to jump out at him at any second.

Rick smiled at that, amused. When he opened the door to the SUV a young girl of about sixteen fell out and landed in his arms.

"Whoa, hey you guys wanna help me here?" Rick called to Greg and Bub. The two men hurried over and Bub reached down and extricated her from the very dead zombie. Her lap was covered in blood and for the moment no one knew if it was hers or the ghouls.

"Let's get her inside where it's safe and then we'll have a look at her. There's a first aid kit back in the station, too."

Bub moved to Rick's side and picked the girl up with ease. Looking down at her, Bub noticed her move slightly in his arms.

"She's coming around, I think," Bub said, walking across the street, to return to the police station.

Greg paused in the street and Rick turned to look at him.

"What's the matter? You coming?" Rick inquired.

Greg nodded yes but pointed to the old lady, still trying to crawl on the asphalt

"What about that? Shouldn't we do something about her?" Greg asked, staring at the crawling body.

"Like what, kill her? You can if you want to, but I've had enough for one day, thanks." Then he turned and followed Bub back to the station.

Greg watched the old woman crawling across the street. At the rate she was moving it would take her nearly half a day to get to the steps of the police station. Greg decided that gave them all plenty of time to worry about it later.

He started back to the station as well, making sure to give himself enough space from those skeleton-like hands.

When he was clear of her, he picked up his pace and in no time was running up the stone steps of the station. The front doors slamming shut behind him.

For the time being, the four survivors were safe, while across the town of Wakefield the fires continued to burn and the dead continued to feed.

Chapter 20

John sat at his desk while Lisa sat in the corner of the lobby feeding baby Vincent. Luckily there had been a half gallon of milk in the second floor break room and even now baby Vincent was sucking it down greedily through a sippy straw.

At first Lisa had trouble getting the baby to drink, as he was used to drinking from a baby bottle with a nipple on the end, but soon the child had adapted and began drinking heartily.

A few hours had passed since Lisa had first arrived and the woman seemed to be looking better. She hadn't had much time to focus on past events since her first duty was the welfare of her child.

John looked to the front doors where the ghouls still congregated. He wasn't sure, but he thought there was a few more in number than earlier in the day, but it was hard to keep track of the shifting bodies.

Dusk covered the town and bathed the lobby in an eerie glow as the sensors turned on the exterior lights outside the building.

John stood up and walked over to Lisa.

"Hey, would you come with me? I want to show you something," John said, moving to the elevator.

Lisa silently followed, baby Vincent cooing in her arms.

The two of them stepped into the elevator and rode to the twelfth floor.

Upon stepping out, John escorted her to the glass windows on the far wall.

"I was up here earlier and it didn't look good, so I thought I'd see how it is now that's its getting dark. From up here you can get a pretty good view of most of the town," John told her while he gazed out across the now darkened landscape.

Lisa looked as well. "Wow, what a view." Then she frowned. "Look at all the fires, why isn't the fire department putting them out?" She inquired.

John just shrugged. "Don't know, really. The news says the emergency response is down to nothing. The crazies out there are attacking anyone they find. They said the police and fire services were the first ones to go. There are power outages all across the eastern seaboard and some of the Midwest. Apparently whatever's happening is spreading."

"Do you think it was terrorists? Maybe it was some kind of biological attack, you know, like the Anthrax scare a few years ago," Lisa said, while staring at the flames. It was almost hypnotic how the orange and red flames would blow in the wind. As she watched, she noticed that entire neighborhoods appeared to be burning. Luckily, where they were was a wide open office park, so even if the conflagration continued it would burn out on its own long before it could ever reach their office building.

Looking straight down she could see the people milling about the front doors.

John followed her gaze and looked as well. From this vantage point it was easier to count the bodies and he could definitely tell there were more people than before.

With a sigh, he turned to walk back to the elevator. "Come on, let's go back down. I'll turn on the news and we can see if anything's getting better."

She nodded, and with one last glance over the town she had lived in with her perfect family, she joined him in the elevator.

*   *   *

The elevator ride was in silence. The two of them each lost in his or her thoughts. The elevator had just passed the fifth floor when the car suddenly lurched to a halt, sending the two of them falling to the floor.

Lisa turned her body and cushioned her baby from the fall, John falling heavily next to her.

The car was plunged into darkness and for a moment John could feel the panic rise in his gut. But then the emergency lights kicked on and he breathed a sigh of relief. Being trapped in an elevator was one thing, but to be trapped in a pitch black elevator was quite another.

Reaching for the handrail, he pulled himself to a standing position and looked around, his eyes falling on Lisa.

"You guys all right?"

Lisa nodded yes. "We're fine, what the hell happened?"

"I'd guess the power went out. Guess we should have taken the stairs, huh?" He said.

"The stairs? That's not funny, John, we're trapped in here and there's nobody to help us." She said, her voice moving up in pitch as she started to panic.

"We could die in here!" She yelled, holding her baby close. The baby sensed its mother's emotions and started to fuss, getting ready for a full blown tirade of screaming.

"All right, just calm down, I took a class in elevator mishaps and I should be able to get us out of here. Do you think you could help me?"

"How, what do you want me to do?"

John pointed to the ceiling. "See that hatch? It leads up to the shaft we're in, and if I can get up there, I should be able to pry open the doors to the floor we're closest to."

"Fine, let's go then," Lisa said, clearly agitated.

"Okay, can you put Vincent down in the corner and give me a boost?"

Reluctantly, Lisa placed Vincent on the floor and with the two of them fussing and heaving, John was able to get a hand on the hatch and push it open, then with a hand up from Lisa, he was able to climb up inside the shaft.

It was pitch black inside the shaft, with only the wan light from the emergency light in the car filtering up to enable him to see.

After a moment his eyes adjusted more and he was able to see the outline of the doors leading to the fifth or sixth floor.

Leaning forward, being careful not to slip and fall down the shaft between the car and the wall, he stuck his fingers between the vertical crack where the two doors connected in the middle. Then with a lot of heaves and ho's, he was able to open the doors exactly one inch.

Lisa stood under the opening in the ceiling and called up to him.

"How's it going, any luck?"

John paused for a moment, breathing heavily and looking at his handiwork. He'd been working at the door for almost an hour and only had it open an inch.

"It's going great. A few more minutes and I should have it open," he lied.

"That's great, John, because I didn't want to say anything, but Vincent just left me a present in his diaper and I would like to change him as soon as possible."

The odor of strained peas and poo wafted up the opening and assailed John's nose. "Wow, healthy kid you got there," he said, waving his hand in front of his nose.

John felt he now had an extra incentive to get the doors open and went back to it with a renewed fervor.

Within the next hour, he slowly was able to get the doors open more. And once he was able to use his legs, as well, he knew he was going to do it.

Then something snapped and fell down the shaft and the doors flew open.

"All right, yeah! Lisa I did it, we're free!" He yelled, proud of himself.

"That's great, John." She congratulated him. "So, can we go? I really need to use the bathroom."

Now that she brought the subject up, John realized he had to go, too. Reaching into the hatch, he was able to grab Lisa's hand. Then he pulled as hard as he could. Luckily Lisa was petite and couldn't weigh more than a hundred and twenty pounds, soaking wet. When he had her up to the lip, he reached his other hand under her shoulder and pulled her up. The whole time Lisa had Vincent in her arms, the baby sleeping quietly.

When she was on top of the car with him, he helped her over the ledge and onto the fifth floor. Then he jumped over as well. Falling to the floor, he sighed in relief.

"Wow, that was close, I was starting to worry there for a while, and then the linkage broke. If the linkage to the door didn't finally bend and break I don't know what we would've done."

"What! Why didn't you say that before?" Lisa asked.

"All macho bravado, babe, let the women think you've got it under control even when you're going down in flames."

Lisa smiled at that and playfully kicked him in the ribs.

"Well, I don't like it. I would've wanted to know exactly what was going on."

"Okay, I'll tell you what; the next time we're both stuck in an elevator together, I'll keep you in the loop the entire time, deal?"

She looked down at him and smiled, after all, he had rescued them. "Deal," she said.

John rolled to his feet. "All right then, let's go back to the lobby."

Before he went to the stairwell, he took a quick look out the window in the hall. He wasn't as high as before, but he could still see a fair amount of the town. More than half the town had lost power.

John had no way of knowing a truck had lost control when the driver had been besieged by rampaging ghouls and had plowed straight into one of the main transformers for half the town.

Seeing the town wreathed in darkness, with nothing but the out of control fires to illuminate the night, he sighed wearily. All that stuff was beyond his power to control, so he decided not to worry about it.

With one last glance out the window, he turned and ushered Lisa into the stairwell for their quiet walk to the lobby.

Chapter 21

Greg slammed the front door of the police station closed and threw the lock.

He turned to see Bub laying the girl down on a nearby desk, the refuse from the top of the desk now lying in a pile on the floor, forgotten. A moment later, Rick dashed into the room with wet paper towels and a small, first aid kit.

Greg walked over to the unconscious girl, as well.

"How's she doin'?" Greg asked, looking down at her.

Rick and Bub were busy wiping her face and neck of blood. Rick was pleased to see that when the blood was wiped away, there were no signs of any open wounds on the girl's body.

"Looks like all the blood was from the nut in the car with her," Rick said, reaching for another clean towel.

"Yeah, looks like we got there just in time. Nice shot by the way," Bub said while cleaning the girl's neck.

"Thanks, I was one of the best in my graduating class," Rick said. He'd begun to clean up the mess from the floor and desk, now that it was clear the girl was okay. Her chest rose and fell steadily, like she was in a deep sleep.

Bub picked her up gently and started to carry her downstairs.

"Where are you bringing her?" Greg asked.

"I figured I'd put her in a cell on one of the cots, at least 'till she comes around." Bub said from the top step. Then he started down the stairs, his heavy footsteps echoing off the walls.

Greg looked to Rick. "Well, what do we do now?"

Rick looked back. "Shit, beats me, I'm just making it up as I go."

Greg headed for the bathroom. "I'm gonna get cleaned up."

Rick waved and headed for the break room. There was a small fridge with milk and bottled water. Reaching for one of the waters he cracked the cap and drank deep, pausing only long enough to take a few deep breaths, then he finished off the bottle.

Leaving the room, he made sure to toss the plastic bottle in the blue tub in the corner. Above the tub was a small sign that said: Wakefield recycles; plastic only.

Then he strolled out into the main room. He thought he'd check the front door and make sure the coast was clear. Moving across the room, he stuck his head up to where the once glass window had filled the door.

Before he could look outside a head appeared in front of him, causing him to jump back and fall onto his butt in surprise.

He let out a short scream, which he would later deny having issued from his mouth, and looked up into the face of a balding middle aged man.

But the thing that calmed Rick down was the blue uniform the man was wearing; a policeman's uniform. Rick just hoped the man wasn't crazy.

While Rick sat on the floor looking up at the man's face in the window, the man spoke.

"Well, Proby, are you gonna let me in or do I have to shoot the lock off?" The policeman asked.

Rick climbed to his feet, knowing everything he needed to know in that one sentence.

Since he had graduated from the academy, all the old timers had called him *Proby*, on account of his probation before he was fully accepted by the other cops. If the man in front of him was using that nickname, then he sure as hell wasn't one of the crazies running around out there in the streets.

Rick smiled. "No, sir, I'll let you in, hold on a sec," he said, climbing to his feet and moving back to the door.

Opening it, the Sergeant he'd last seen at the mortuary stepped inside the station.

His once blue uniform was covered in blood and he had a rip on his right shirtsleeve; the man holding it tight against his body.

He moved into the station and Rick closed the door, double checking to make sure it was clear.

It wasn't.

On top of the ones they'd killed, six more had arrived and Rick had to wonder if more would come after them.

The station might have been a good fall back position, but probably wasn't good for a long term place of safety.

But the question was; where was a safe place to go?

His thoughts were disturbed by the Sergeant. The man had literally dropped into a chair, all the strength leaving him now that he knew he was safe.

Rick moved over to him and gave the man one of the wet towels still on a nearby desk.

"Shit, Sarge, it's good to see at least one other cop. I thought I was the only one left," Rick said.

"You probably are, son. I barely got out of there alive. Shit, one of them still got a piece of me" he said, holding up his wounded arm. A small one inch piece of meat was missing, the blood already clotting. "I could use a little help getting bandaged up, though."

Rick paused for a second and then nodded. "Sure, Sarge, just stay put, I'll go get the first aid kit again and I'll fix you up," Rick said moving off to the other room where the kit was stored.

He returned less than a minute later. On top of the kit, he'd brought the Sergeant a bottle of water. Handing it to the exhausted man, he drank it down quickly, the overflow spilling down the front of his bloody shirt.

When he finished he set the bottle down, wiping his mouth with the back of his good hand. "Thanks, Proby... that hit the spot. What did you mean about the first aid kit, is some one else hurt?"

"Rick shook his head no. "No, Sarge, we saved a civilian girl from those nuts outside and we thought she might have been hurt. She wasn't though."

Rick had the peroxide out and was ready to pour it over the Sergeant's wound.

"You ready for this? It's gonna sting a little."

The Sarge nodded for Rick to go for it.

Rick poured the bottle over the ripped flesh and the wound immediately began to bubble and foam.

The Sergeant gritted his teeth and squirmed in his chair, the pain clearly excruciating. After a few minutes, the spasms subsided and Rick started to wrap the arm with surgical gauze. With the foam surrounding the wound, Rick didn't see the small worms that burrowed deeper into the Sergeant's arm, trying to escape the peroxide. Nor did the Sarge realize he had unwanted houseguests in his body.

With the wound wrapped, Rick stood back and inspected his handiwork.

"How's that feel?"

The Sarge flexed his hand. "Okay, I guess. Still hurts like a bastard, though."

"Well, you should get to a hospital and have the emergency room look at it," Rick said. Then he noticed Greg standing by the bathroom door.

The young man had decided to stand quiet until Rick had been done with the Sergeant's arm. Now he walked over to the two policemen.

"Hey, I'm Greg. It's good to see another officer."

"Yeah, well, I'm probably it. Those crazy bastards out there are jumping us and killing us as fast as we show up. And get this, bullets don't stop them. They just shrug them off like some kind of zombie. And it gets worse. I saw some of my men go down under a pile of those things and later when they were most definitely dead, my men got back up again and then they started to attack the rest of us. When it got down to me being the last one alive, I decided I'd done my duty. Besides, I couldn't help anyone if I was dead. So I beat feet, and ran for the station. The hospitals are overrun with wounded and I hear the infection is spreading there, too. Believe me, the last place you'd want to be right now is a hospital. I tell ya, I don't know what the hell is going on in the world right now, but it's some bad shit."

The Sergeant leaned back in his chair and rested, while Rick and Greg looked at each other.

"Great, what the hell are we gonna do?" Greg asked whoever was listening.

"I say we stay here for now, those things can't get inside and we have plenty of ammo. What do you say, Sarge?"

The Sergeant was falling asleep, last night and today finally catching up to him.

Rick hit Greg in the arm to get his attention.

"Come on, get his legs and I'll get his arms. Let's put him in the Captain's office, he's got a couch in there."

Greg nodded and the two men picked the Sergeant up and crab-walked him to the office. Rick almost dropped his half of the body when he tried to open the office door, but then he got it open and the two men, with the dead weight between them, stumbled into the office. They dropped the Sergeant, more then they laid him, onto the couch, the exhausted man never even stirring.

Then the two men left, leaving the door ajar an inch or so as they went downstairs to see how their newest acquisition was doing.

*   *   *

The Sergeant stirred fitfully on the couch while the worms continued to infect his body. Some of the parasites had already made it to the man's heart where they proceeded to feed.

An hour later, the Sergeant sat up, grabbed his chest in pain, and then fell back to the couch in his death throes. The worms had already eaten parts of his spine and nerves, in effect paralyzing the man, the spasm he'd just experienced being his last.

While the small group of survivors went about their business downstairs in the cell area, the Sergeant was slowly dying, his body already falling into a deep coma that he would never awaken from. The parasites continued feeding; doing what instinct told them to do.

Soon the Sergeant would die and then return as one of the walking dead.

As the hours went by and night fell, the survivors got ready for bed, confident in the fact they were secure in the police station.

But unknowingly, they had brought death into the very place they had fought so hard to keep safe; and only time would tell if any of them would see the sunrise again.

Chapter 22

John slowed down on the last few stairs before the door that would lead him back into the lobby. Placing his finger to his lips, he bade Lisa be quiet.

"You hear that?" He asked her.

"Hear what? I don't hear anything," Lisa said. Her feet hurt. It had been a long walk down the five flights of stairs and her leg muscles hurt, the calves feeling like she had just done an hour on the treadmill.

The noise drifted through the door again; a moaning sound.

"What the hell could that be?" John asked, perplexed.

Deciding it was nothing; he went to the stairwell door and opened it out to the lobby.

He wasn't even past the door, when he slammed on the brakes, turned and backed up into the stairwell again, pushing Lisa with him.

"What the hell, John, be careful of Vincent," she chastised him.

"Sorry, Lisa, but we got big problems. The front doors are shattered and those bastards have gotten in. If we go out there, we're dead."

"Really? Let me see."

At his disapproving look she added: "Don't worry, I wont let them see me. Here, take Vincent," she said, handing the baby to John.

John had never been good with children and he held the baby at arms length, not quite comfortable with the situation he now found himself in.

While John dealt with Vincent, Lisa had gone to the stairwell door and opened it just enough for her right eye to peek through.

It wasn't good. The front doors were indeed shattered, the glass littering the floor, with only moonlight and the emergency lighting illuminating the lobby. The entire lobby was filled with what Lisa could only think to call raving maniacs. Their bloody clothes and terrible wounds to their bodies only added to the macabre picture.

They were indeed trapped. The front doors were too far away and they wouldn't get more than ten feet before they were overwhelmed.

Backing away from the door, she turned back to John. The second she was finished, he handed the baby back to her, relieved that his ordeal was over.

Lisa cradled Vincent in her arms.

"Well, satisfied?" He asked.

She nodded yes. "What are we gonna do now? We're stuck in here with no food or water and the lights are out.

John shrugged. "Beats the hell out of me, I'm kinda new to all this chaos, myself. Why don't you come up with an idea?" He quipped back.

"What about the back door? Surely you have one."

John shook his head from side to side. "No good, we'd still have to fight our way around the desk and then we'd be on foot. We need to get to my car, or better yet, the security pickup parked next to it."

Lisa stood still, thinking. John noticed her eyebrows would scrunch up whenever she was concentrating on something. He found himself becoming attracted to her. He knew he shouldn't be attracted to anyone at a time like this, but he couldn't help himself.

John found his eyes were gazing over her petite body, her shoulder length brown hair which was just caressing the top of her shoulders. Despite everything she'd been through she still looked remarkably appealing.

Pushing those thoughts down below in his mind for another time; he averted his eyes when she looked up at him. But then he noticed she was looking past him. He turned to see nothing behind him but the red fire extinguisher.

"What? What are you looking at?" He asked, confused.

She pointed to the fire extinguisher. "That. We can use the fire extinguisher to distract those maniacs. In the foam and mist we should be able to run for the doors," she said, pleased with herself.

John mulled it over for a while. It wasn't a half bad idea and frankly, he had nothing better.

"Okay, let's do it," he said, pulling the red cylinder off the wall. He checked the pressure gauge and grunted when he saw it was in the green; a full can.

"All right, on three, I'll go first and spray the hell out of 'em. You run for the security truck. My keys are in my jacket pocket on the back of the chair at the desk. I should be able to grab it on my way out."

He moved to the door and cracked it an inch. The lobby was full of bodies, the people shambling about without purpose.

John stood there for a moment, trying to psych himself up. He wasn't a hero, never had been. But then, he had never really been in a situation when his character was put to the test to this extreme.

Taking one more look over his shoulder at Lisa, he smiled.

"Okay, one, two...three!" He yelled, kicking the door open and charging into the lobby. From where the stairwell door was, they were away from most of the ghouls. The second the couple stepped into the open, the undead crowd turned and began moving towards them.

John was ready.

When the first ghoul came within reach, he blasted it with the foam from the extinguisher. The pale face was covered in white, for the moment becoming blind. Not realizing it, the ghoul attacked one of its brethren, mistaking the other one for prey. While the two fought each other, John took a step forward.

The next one in line got a blast in the face, as well, and then John swung the back of the canister into the foam-covered face, crushing the foamy countenance until red began to mix with the white bubbles.

Three more zombies stood in front of him and he held the spicket high and sprayed their faces in a sweeping motion from side to side.

He continued doing this until he'd made it past them. Lisa had made a run for it at the first sign of an opening and now she stood at the security truck, anxiously waiting for him to catch up.

He just had to grab his coat with his keys and he'd be home free.

He reached over the desk; while behind him the ghouls stumbled into each other blind. He grabbed the collar and began to pull the jacket to him.

Suddenly, a child's head popped out from under the desk and tried to take a bite out of his arm.

His reflexes sharp, he pulled his arm away from the biting jaws, the child's teeth snapping down on empty air. Then the child crawled out and climbed onto the desk. Before John could even move, the child leaped at him, both of them falling to the floor.

The child couldn't have been more than ten or eleven, but the wiggling, twisting body was unstoppable. Teeth snapped at his face and neck, while he tried to keep the child at bay. John didn't want to hurt the boy, but the child was leaving him little choice.

On the next attack of teeth, John decided he'd had enough. He pulled his right hand back and slapped the boy's face with a resounding whack!

The dead boy reeled back for a second, the force of the blow stunning him, and then he turned his head back to lean over John, the blood from a split cheek draining from his mouth to drip onto John's chest.

John heard movement close by and looked up as some of the zombies came for him, most of the foam clear of their eyes.

With a heave, John bucked his hips, sending the child flying off him, where the boy's head struck the corner of the desk with a muffled thump.

Despite the peril he was in, John couldn't help but panic. If the child was mortally wounded, how would he explain it to the police, when they finally arrived?

But his worry was for nothing, because a second later, the boy stood up and with crimson eyes flashing in the gloom of the lobby, prepared to attack John again.

In the dim light, John was still able to see the two-inch dent in the side of the child's pale forehead where wood and flesh had battled and the flesh had lost.

John only had the briefest moment to wonder how the boy could still be functioning with half his head dented in, when the child came at him again.

John reached out and pulled the extinguisher to him and sprayed the foam into the boy's face, then after retrieving his jacket, yet again, he bolted for the front doors, almost slipping on the glass littering the lobby floor.

Just before he was through the doors, a ghoul came at him from his side. He didn't even think about his next move, he just acted. With the ghoul lunging towards him, he brought up the extinguisher and slammed it into the dead man's face. Cartilage collapsed and the nose flattened as the bottom of the canister pulverized the pale visage.

The living corpse went down, for the moment dazed, its eyes covered with mashed flesh.

John didn't wait around for round two. Dropping the fire extinguisher, he jumped through the shattered front doors and sprinted for Lisa and his truck.

When he was at the truck, his hand dove into his jacket pocket in search of his keys. Fingers searched valiantly and his heart started to crawl up his throat when he realized they weren't in the jacket.

Then he paused and checked the other pocket of the jacket. The moment his hand dug into his pocket, his fingers felt the cold metal of his keys.

Feeling stupid, he pulled them out and opened his door, while Lisa ran around to the passenger side.

The door opened and John jumped in while opening the locks for Lisa.

No sooner had he closed his door then a bloody, foamy face slammed into his the window. He yelled out from the shock, realizing they weren't safe yet, not by a long shot, as his father used to say.

Lisa screamed next to him and Vincent began crying, as well. On top of that, the ghoul was growling and banging on the window, others close behind.

The noise was deafening and he thought he was probably screaming too, and didn't even realize it.

He slammed the ignition key into its home, the six cylinders roaring to life. By now the zombies had surrounded the truck and were starting to climb into the bed in back. John didn't hesitate. Slamming the transmission in reverse, he floored the pedal, the ghouls in the back bed, flying over the cab of the truck to land on the asphalt. Others were knocked down and John rode over them like speed bumps. Flesh and gore became imbedded into the treads of the tires as he drove over them and then turned to drive off.

Placing the truck in drive, he noticed he was clear of bodies for the immediate moment, except for one man in a Halloween costume (he thought it was once a clown suit) who was standing directly in front of the truck about five feet away.

With nothing but the stars and the half moon for light, John distinctly saw the man's blood-red eyes gleaming in the night.

"The hell with this shit. I've had it with these bastards. Up 'till now I've really tried not to hurt anyone, but screw it, if he won't move, then I'm going through him," John muttered while Lisa sat next to him, terrified, hugging Vincent in her arms.

John pulled the knob for his headlights, the white light blinding the ghoul. He slammed his foot on the gas pedal and the engine roared to life, but then stalled. The pickup rolled the few feet towards the ghoul and stopped just as the front bumper touched the swaying corpse.

Lisa looked at John with terror in her eyes but, John just smiled, embarrassed.

"Sorry, it's not a new truck," he said, quietly.

Placing the car in park, he started the engine again. On the second try, the engine roared to life. He revved it for a second to make sure it was going to continue to run and then stepped on the gas, albeit with a little less pressure than before. The ghoul was pushed out of the way by the thousands of pounds of metal and John continued down the long driveway.

A few zombies tried to latch onto the sides of the vehicle, but soon let go when the truck picked up speed, the bodies tumbling to the pavement in a heap of rolling limbs and heads.

John looked in his rearview mirror to see dim shapes in the dark. When he reached the main street he took a quick left and headed deeper in to the town. From earlier in the day, he knew Route-95 was hopelessly clogged with vehicles.

His only hope would be to try and make it through the town and then cross into Melrose. Then if his luck held, he could drive home from there. Or if it was bad there, too, maybe he could continue into Malden and then loop around the long way.

He slowed down and drove around an abandoned garbage truck, then continued on.

The maniacs were everywhere, running around or just standing in place. As the truck would drive by them, they would start to follow it and would only stop when John turned a corner and was lost from their view.

The roads were clogged with cars and trucks and sometimes John had to drive on the sidewalk just to get around the wrecks.

Many of the houses they passed were on fire, as well, some no more than blackened husks after the fire was spent.

Vincent was crying in Lisa's arms and John looked at them both, Lisa frowning deeply.

"He's probably hungry. I have to feed him, but I don't have any formula."

John gazed around the street they were on. He didn't think there were any stores in the area where he could get milk or baby formula. He drove on, wracking his brain for an idea, when he slowed the truck in front of a cozy, little, white house.

In the front lawn by the door was a playpen. John pulled into the driveway, and after making sure the coast was clear, turned off the engine.

"Why are we stopping? Do you know these people?" Lisa asked, looking around her and at the house specifically.

John shook his head no and pointed at the front door, which was open wide and blowing back and forth in the wind.

"No, I don't know them, but with that playpen in the yard they must have young kids and with the door open I doubt if anybody's home."

Lisa looked around the area. "It doesn't look like the power's on around here, though. Look, no lights. Not even the street lamps are on. Just like at your building."

John nodded, and with the creaking of the vehicle's door hinges, he opened it and climbed out. The two of them moved quietly up the driveway and over the perfectly cut and edged lawn, until they'd reached the front door.

John reached for the swinging door, stopping its motion with his hand. Then, with a look at Lisa for emotional support, the two of them stepped into the darkened house.

*   *   *

Below in the basement, two crimson eyes flared.

The newly revived ghoul had heard the creaking of floorboards when the prey entered its home.

But this one was patient.

While above on the first floor, John and Lisa explored, down below their feet a zombie licked its lips.

The man who had once lived in this house with his family was hungry again. Below him, littering the cellar floor, were the remains of his wife and child.

He had turned after being attacked by a dog while putting out the trash for sidewalk pickup. He had then entered his house and attacked his wife. So much of her had been eaten in the past day there was nothing left for the worms to reanimate. When he was finished with her, he'd heard the wails of his one year son coming from the first floor. Not too much later, that soul, also, had been extinguished. He'd then dragged their bodies into the cellar, the dark cool air pleasant to him.

But now he was out of food, the meat on the two bodies all but gone. Nothing now left but tattered bits of flesh and gnawed bones.

He began moving quietly up the stairs with stiff legs. The prey was so close and he could already taste their tender flesh.

Chapter 23

Rick glanced up and gazed around the room from the desk and chair that had become his bed for the night, the others all fast asleep.

There had only been the cells with their three beds available, so Rick had volunteered to sleep at the duty desk across from the cells.

He looked at his wristwatch, the fluorescent hands telling him it was just after two in the morning. Despite his sleeping position, it hadn't taken him long to fall asleep, the rigors of the past two days finally catching up to him.

His back reminded him he hadn't slept in a bed for the past forty-eight hours and he stood up to work out the kinks.

His ears picked up the sounds of squeaking floorboards and he looked up at the ceiling. The only person upstairs was the Sarge and the last time he'd seen him the man had been fast asleep. In fact, the man seemed to be sleeping the sleep of the dead.

Rick decided to investigate, forgetting his .45, which had been placed on the desk when he'd gone to sleep hours earlier.

Not really knowing why, he quietly made his way to the first floor. The room was illuminated by the fires still burning from across the street; the fluorescent lights off.

Moving to the light switches, he flicked them up and down to negative results.

"Shit," he whispered to himself. While the group had slept the power had gone out.

He heard something scrape a desk across the room and he stopped messing with the light switch. A shape moved by in the twilight of shadows.

"Hey, Sarge, that you?" He whispered.

In response, the shape moved closer to him, still not talking.

His spidey sense started tingling and he placed his hand on his gun, cursing silently upon realizing it was downstairs.

"Come on, Sarge, if that's you, you need to say something. You're scaring the hell out of me."

The shape moved closer until the figure was no more than three feet away.

Squinting in the darkness, Rick tried to make out the face. Then the figure moved forwards another foot, the face moving into a streak of light falling from a side window.

At first Rick breathed a sigh of relief when he saw it was the Sergeant, but then he was able to make out the man's face better and realized something was definitely wrong with him. For one thing, his complexion was a pale, waxy color and his expression was one of a slack jawed, drug-induced hippie.

The Sergeant turned his face more towards Rick and that's when he felt the panic begin to grow. In the gloom of the station, the Sarge's eyes gleamed dull red, reminding Rick of all the crazies running around town.

"Oh, Christ, not you, too," Rick gasped. He wanted to say more, but wasn't able because the Sarge had turned and was lunging towards him.

Instinctively, Rick put his hands out in front of himself, and the gesture was the only thing that saved his life.

While the Sergeant tried his best to sink his teeth into Rick's jugular, Rick had his hands between the two of them and was just barely fending the larger man off.

"Don't do this, Sarge, please," Rick pleaded as he fought the man off.

All around them, chairs were overturned and miscellaneous clutter on desktops fell to the floor while the two men stumbled around the precinct.

Rick desperately looked for some kind of weapon, but none could be found. Not that he would have the opportunity to retrieve one. The Sarge's attack was unrelenting, the man continually trying to take a bite out of Rick.

The back of Rick's leg struck a fallen chair and the man went crashing to the wooden floor with the Sergeant on top of him.

The impact sent the air rushing from his lungs, the Sergeant's leg accidentally crushing Rick's testicles. The young cop saw stars, the pain blinding him for a second.

That second was all the time the Sergeant needed to rip Rick's flesh apart. The older man's head dove at Rick's throat, but came up short a fraction of an inch.

Then the infected man was pulled away from Rick and sent flying across the room, where he landed on a desk and rolled to the floor.

Rick's eye's had closed from the expected pain, and when he now opened them, he saw the smiling face of Bub leaning over him.

Bub put one of his massive hands under Rick and heaved the smaller man to his feet in one smooth pull.

"You all right, there, partner? Looks like your cop buddy was about to make you a late night snack," Bub said, casting a glance over to where the Sarge had fallen. As of yet, the man was still down.

Rick looked around dazed. "Yeah, I think I'm okay. He tried to bite me, why'd he do that?" Rick asked Bub.

Bub shrugged. "Shit if I know, maybe he's infected with whatever the others got."

A rustling sound had both men looking to where the Sergeant had fallen. They watched the man pull himself to his feet, except now one arm was at an impossible angle.

"Ouch, that's gotta hurt," Bub said, watching the wounded cop stumble around the desk and start towards the two men again.

"Doesn't seem to be bothering him too much," Rick stated, moving back a little. "Tell you what, Bub. Why don't you take care of this and we'll call it even with the whole thing of you being in jail."

Bub glanced over at Rick. "Yeah? Deal. What about this guy? What do you wanna do with him? I guess we could kill him," Bub suggested.

Rick shook his head adamantly no. "No way, he's my superior, I don't want to have to explain any of this when other cops finally show up. Can we throw him in one of the cells for now? At least he can't hurt anyone in there."

Bub shrugged subtly. "Sure, man, whatever."

The Sarge was only four feet away by now and he continued forward, undaunted by the size of Bub.

Bub towered over the sergeant by at least a foot and had to have at least fifty pounds on the dead cop.

When the Sarge was close enough, Bub sent a right cross into the man's mouth that sent teeth flying across the room. The Sarge's face seemed to deflate from the impact, his head rocking to the side with his body soon following.

Before the dead cop could regain his balance, Bub had jumped on top of the walking corpse, and with some phone wire from a nearby desk, began to wrap the Sarge's hands behind his back. The entire time the trapped dead man continued to try and bite any piece of flesh that came near him.

"He's persistent, I'll give him that," Bub said.

Once Bub had the Sergeant secured, he pulled him to his feet again.

"Hey, Rick, you got any duct tape around here?"

Rick thought about it for a second and then ran off to a closet in the back of the station. A half minute later, he returned with a roll of black duct tape in his hands.

"One of the guys on the nightshift brought it in when he needed to fix his radiator hose. He said this stuff will fix anything in a pinch."

"Hell, yeah, I had a 1978 Buick Skylark that was nothing more than an engine, duct tape and a set of tires."

Bub took the roll from Rick and ripped off a good sized piece and then stuck it over the Sarge's mouth. The cop's head flared around ineffectually, but for the moment, he was definitely neutralized.

"There. That should hold him and prevent him from biting anyone," Bub turned the Sarge around and waved his finger at the dead man.

"Didn't your mother ever tell you it's not nice to bite?"

Greg's voice floated up to them from the ground floor.

"Is everything okay up there?" He called.

"Yeah, it's cool, just stay there, we'll be down in a minute," Bub said. He glanced over to Rick and smiled. "When we heard all the commotion, I told him to stay down there and keep an eye on the girl."

Rick nodded, understanding. "Oh, okay."

Bub moved for the steps, pushing the Sergeant in front of him. The dead man fought Bub the entire time, but was no match for Bub's superior size and soon captor and captive were moving down the stairs.

Rick hung back for a moment and said: "I just want to see how the street is doing. I don't wanna become trapped in here with no way out."

"Yeah, sure, but come downstairs when you're done," Bub told him and then his head disappeared down the stairs.

Rick moved to the front door and searched outside for any problems.

The stars were out and covered the night sky like a shimmering carpet. Their light, plus the half moon, was the only illumination covering the debris strewn road. Well, that and the fires from the burning houses.

Rick gazed at the street and the people milling about. He looked down at the front steps through the hole where the glass used to be in the front door and was surprised to see the old lady from earlier in the day.

She had managed to crawl across the street and was now at the bottom of the steps. Behind her was a red trail of blood and skin. The woman's body had been rubbed raw as she pulled herself along the rough asphalt. As for the others in the street, they didn't know anyone was in the police station and were ignoring it. Rick could only hope that continued.

Off to the side of the station, he saw the bright light of the fires that had been burning through the night.

If the flames weren't extinguished soon, then it was a real possibility the entire town could go up in one massive bonfire.

Turning away from the doors with a sigh, he moved to the stairs and descended back to the ground floor. He wanted to make sure the Sarge was okay. Whatever had happened wasn't the man's fault and Rick wanted to make sure he was safe for as long as he was able.

*   *   *

Tommy had found another house no more than a block from the police station. It was a cute little duplex with flowers along the walk and window boxes on all the windows.

But the best thing Tommy loved about this particular building was what it said to him. It called to him and begged him to set it on fire. The house wanted to feel the caressing flames of the inferno as it was consumed.

Tommy stood in front of the house with a lighter in one hand and one of his gas cans in the other.

After the incident with the matches, he'd decided to upgrade to a lighter, not wanting to take the chance with matches again.

This would be the twelfth fire tonight he'd started. But that was fine with him. He'd been repressing these urges all his life and now was able to let it loose, like the flames he was so enamored with.

Looking around and relieved there were no crazies in the immediate area, he decided to get to work before any popped up.

With a smile on his face and a skip in his step, he walked to the front door. He needed to get moving. There were many more buildings calling to him, he just hadn't found them yet. But he knew before the sun rose once again, he would find them all...and burn them.

Chapter 24

John and Lisa stepped into the kitchen of the small house. John closed the door behind him and nearly walked into Lisa. He was about to ask her what was wrong when he saw for himself.

The kitchen floor and some of the cabinets were covered in blood. Partially dried red rivulets ran down the wooden cabinets and pooled on the worn linoleum.

What was strange was there was no sign of the bodies the blood had obviously come from.

Vincent wined in Lisa's arms, making her forget about the blood and look for some food for her child.

With nothing but the twilight outside to illuminate the kitchen, she moved to the refrigerator. The power may have been off, but it hadn't been that long and she was sure the food wouldn't have spoiled yet.

Her assumption was correct; the milk was still a little cold. While she prepared Vincent's meal, John moved off into the dining room to inspect the house. It was neat and clean, the furniture worn but well kept.

There was a picture on the mantle and John went over and looked at it. Picking it up, he walked over to the window to see the picture better. The picture looked like it had been taken at a park. The three individuals in the photo looked happy.

Man and wife and baby had nothing to look forward to but the happiness of each other. But then the world seemed to crumble apart from the inside out and now there was blood covering the family's kitchen and at least one of them was probably dead.

He thought of his own ex-wife and wondered if she'd been ripped to bloody shreds by the maniacs now running around the streets. He didn't know if that occurrence would make him happy or sad if it came to pass.

Placing the picture back on the mantle out of some kind of silent respect for another man's home, he moved around some more, exploring.

On the far wall was a set of knives. Actually it was a katana as well as the smaller accompanied pieces, all with the same color sheaths.

He reached for them. While they were more for show than as real battle weapons, he decided they were better than nothing.

He stuck the smaller knife, no more than eight inches long in his back pocket.

The katana he held onto. He pulled it from its sheath, the blade reflecting the dim light in the gloom of the living room. If it worked as well as it looked, then he might have a formidable weapon.

Feeling better with a weapon in his possession, he continued exploring. He was about to go upstairs to make sure the bedrooms were clear when Lisa let out a panicked scream.

Turning, he dashed back to the kitchen, nearly falling over an ottoman in the unfamiliar house. Cursing his throbbing shin, he ran into the kitchen.

He stopped when he saw what had frightened Lisa.

A man had entered the kitchen from a door just off the kitchen, and if John had to guess, he would have assumed the doorway led to a basement or garage; and as he watched in surprise, the man was trying to reach Lisa.

Luckily, she had put the kitchen table between herself and the man and was safe for the moment. With her baby in her hands, and the floor slippery with congealing blood, she tried to maintain her balance and stay away from the ghoul's grasping hands.

John looked at the man and was surprised to see he recognized him. It was the same man in the photo he'd just seen. The man looked very different now, however. His face was covered in blood and his hands were a mess of ripped nails and deep cuts. A piece of his neck had been ripped out and as John watched the man in the wan light, he thought he could see things squirming in the wound.

With John in the kitchen as well, the ghoul didn't know who to go after first.

John took that decision from him in a second. Pulling the katana from its sheath, he held it in front of him like in so many movies he'd seen. The sheath he let fall to the floor. If everything worked out, he could retrieve it later.

"Lisa, stay there, he can't get you," John said, as he turned to the dead man. "Look, buddy, I know this is your house, but we have a baby that needed food. Just let us go and we'll leave. I promise."

The dead man just growled deep in his throat and ran at John in a stumbling, drunken pace. Lisa screamed, Vincent howled and John panicked.

Without thinking it through, he thrust the katana in front of him, the ghoul impaling himself on the blade. Before John realized it, the dead man was face to face with him, the blade sticking out of the guy's back...the man didn't seem to mind.

John pushed the ghoul away from him and stepped back at the same time. The katana slid free like a hot knife through butter, leaving nothing but a rip in the man's already bloody clothes and a small sputter of blood from the wound.

John just stood there. The man should be doubled over in pain, not getting ready to attack him again. Then he remembered the boy at the lobby with the dented head. He, too, didn't seem to mind the mortal wound. Then there was the news broadcasts he'd seen before the power went out.

That's when it all hit him. Somehow the people who were running around crazy were dead, just like the scientist on the television had said. He knew it was the most unbelievable thing in the world to try to believe, but all the facts proved it.

All this went through John's head in a fraction of a second as he stood in front of what he now realized was a zombie.

The ghoul's red eyes flashed malevolently at John and it lunged for him again.

John stepped back and slashed at the exposed neck. The sharp blade cut halfway before stopping. John pulled it free, the dead man's blood spraying over his shoulders to land on the linoleum. The dead man didn't have a lot of blood left after his own attack and the blood just dribbled out the wound and onto his shoes. John brought the sword up again and brought it down in another slashing motion. The blade bit deep into the already half-severed neck and completed what the first slash had begun.

The severed head flew from the ghoul's shoulder to bounce off the cabinet and land in the sink. The body stumbled around for a moment, like a lackluster chicken, and then fell to the floor with a thump, breaking a kitchen chair with the weight of the falling body.

John stood in the middle of the kitchen breathing heavily, blood spray covering his face and security uniform. Lisa ran over to him and buried her head in his shoulder. With his free hand he consoled her, while the other held the dripping, vermilion blade.

She cried for a few minutes and then got hold of herself, her baby giving her strength.

John moved away from her and inspected the body. Tiny worms fell from the wound, looking to John like maggots. He didn't give them a moments thought.

"Why don't I get rid of this," he said, pointing to the headless corpse.

Lisa nodded, not really knowing what to do at the moment; a bit of shock still there.

John dragged the corpse out onto the front lawn, and after making sure the area was clear, he darted back inside the house.

Next he went to the sink, where the hapless head still lay. Scrunching his face in disgust, he grabbed the head by its hair and picked it up. The bodiless face was facing John, and he shrieked like a girl, dropping the head to the floor when the eyes opened and stared at him, the mouth trying to say something.

Lisa looked up frightened again, not knowing why John had screamed, until John was able to get himself together again.

"Sorry, the head just freaked me out a little, everything's fine," he said, embarrassed.

"Good, then would you please get rid of that thing? I don't want it near me," Lisa said while feeding a cup of milk to Vincent. "Or Vincent."

She knew she had to be strong, her baby needed her.

John smiled stupidly and nodded. "Sure, no problem."

He steeled himself and reached for the head again. This time he made sure to keep the face pointed away from him and also away from Lisa's view. He figured she didn't need to see it, not after everything else she'd been through.

With the head at arms length, he walked to the door and opened it. Double checking the street to make sure it was still clear, he opened the door a little more and looked at the head. This time when the eyes looked at him he was ready.

"Look, pal, sorry about cutting off your head and all, but you gave me no choice. I promise to take good care of your house, but you gotta go. See ya."

He tossed the head into the night, the head rolled like an off balance bowling ball, until it came to a stop at the edge of the lawn. By this time John had returned inside with Lisa, not caring where the head ended up.

An hour later, a pack of dogs came roaming by and found the head. The head tried to growl at them, but without vocal cords or air it proved impossible.

One of the animals picked the head up in its bloody teeth and the pack moved on. If live meat couldn't be found than brains would do in a pinch.

Inside the house, the pair of survivors had a meager meal of canned food, and once John had secured the house for the night, they went to bed in one of the upstairs bedrooms.

They knew it wouldn't be wise to stay in the abandoned house permanently, but one night would suffice.

*   *   *

A block away, a house was burning, the wind carrying the embers to adjacent homes. While the embers smoldered, it was just a matter of time before the rest of the structures would be aflame, as well.

With many sections of Wakefield now burning, the ghouls began to migrate away from the encroaching fires.

At the moment, the walking dead were slowly moving across the town and soon would all be in the general vicinity of the police station.

While in the police station, four weary people went about the grim business of surviving, unaware of the troubles to come.

Chapter 25

Greg lay in his cot with eyes wide open, staring at the ceiling like the small pockmarks from tossed pencils were tiny, dark stars.

After the trouble with the Sergeant, he'd finally managed to fall back asleep, but that hadn't lasted for very long.

The Sergeant stood in the cell next to Greg's, nothing but the iron bars keeping the man from attacking him.

Even with his mouth taped closed and his hands tied behind his back, Greg was scared shit of the man. He'd heard what the infected man had done upstairs and didn't have a clue why they were keeping him alive.

If he was to escape, he would immediately try to attack any of the survivors, so why take the chance? He turned on his side to see the girl sleeping soundly. She had come to about an hour after they had rescued her, and after changing into some fresh clothes from the locker room, they had all gathered around as she told them her tale.

Greg still thought back to how he felt when Kim had shared with them about her mother and what had happened. His own mother was hopefully safe in California, although he didn't know exactly how far this madness had spread.

He'd wanted to try and call her, but Rick had told him the phones were out. When the young officer wasn't looking, he'd checked for himself and had heard nothing but dead air.

Now with the power out, they didn't even have light. All the windows on the first floor were open to let in as much illumination as possible; the heights of the frames well out of reach from any people on the ground.

Greg's nose itched from the smell of smoke that drifted in through the open windows. The fires were getting closer and he knew if they didn't get put out then they would all have to abandon their sanctuary for fear of being burned alive.

A muffled growl had Greg looking at the Sergeant again. The man's eyes flashed red as they seemed to bore into Greg's very soul. Deciding he wasn't going to be getting any more sleep, he raised himself up, put his shoes back on and went upstairs.

Bub was sitting at a desk with Rick. Both men were playing cards together by the light of a flickering candle.

"Hey, guys, how's it going?" Greg asked, sitting on a desk next to the two men, his legs swung back and forth under the desk, like he was only eight years old.

"Hey, Greg, what's wrong, can't sleep?" Rick asked.

"Hell, no, not with ugly always growling and staring at me. What's gonna happen to him?" Greg asked.

"Figure we'll just let him stay where he is. Let the next guy worry about him," Bub said, placing his cards on the desk.

"Gin, I win again, Rick. That's another twenty you owe me," Bub said, a smile cutting across his face.

"Sure, Bub, no problem, I'll just stop by an ATM on my way home today. Is tens and twenties all right?" Rick quipped back.

Bub continued smiling while he reshuffled the deck.

Greg hopped down from the desk and went to the front doors. In the gloom of the night, he could see figures moving about. Some of them were sitting in the middle of the street while others appeared to be eating something. Greg turned away, not wanting to know what it might be, but having an idea.

"There's more of them out there," Greg stated, sitting on the desk again.

"Yeah, but they're out there, and we're in here, so it's cool," Bub said. He had finished shuffling the cards and had dealt him and Rick a new hand.

"How's the girl?" Bub asked, placing a card down.

"Okay, I guess. When I came up here she was sleeping again."

Silence hung around the three men for a few minutes as Bub and Rick played gin. Then Greg spoke up again.

"Hey, did you guys smell the smoke? It smells stronger than before. Why the hell isn't the fire department putting out those fires?"

"Probably because there isn't a fire department left anymore to do it," Bub said.

He laid his cards down and looked at Greg and Rick.

"Either of you religious?" Bub inquired.

Rick shook his head no. "Not really. I mean, I was raised Catholic, but I hated going to church and when I was on my own I never felt the need," Rick said.

Bub then looked at Greg.

"Me? Hell no. I guess I'm Protestant, but my parents never went to church, well, except for the usual holidays, like Christmas and Easter. Why?"

"Why? Because what's going on outside is nothing more than the friggin' apocalypse come to life. My dad was a church goin' man and he dragged my ass to church every single Sunday. I don't remember too much about what the priest said, but I do remember the stuff about the end of the world. That's the bad stuff about the four horsemen and plagues and shit. And that's what's happening now. It was gonna happen sooner or later and I guess it's finally gone and happened. Now all we can do is deal with it and try to survive."

Rick and Greg sat there quietly, not really knowing how to respond.

Then Rick said: "Look, Bub, you're entitled to your beliefs, but I can't honestly believe this is the end of the world."

"Then how do you explain the dead walking, Rick?" Bub asked.

"The dead walking? You mean like zombies? What the hell are you talking about?" Greg asked.

Bub pointed to the front doors and beyond.

"When we saved Kim, I shot a guy three times and he barely flinched. I don't care if he was on something. When you get half your chest blown off you are fucking dead. But that guy didn't. I had to shoot him in the head before he finally went down for good. Now if that isn't the definition of a goddamn zombie, then I don't his chest. To him the conversation was over.

"Jesus, Bub, zombies? You can't be serious," Rick said.

"Just think about all the weird shit you've seen recently and then get back to me. Then you'll see I'm right," Bub said.

Greg hopped off the desk and walked to the bathroom. "What's next, vampires and werewolves? Oh, lookout, I just saw a mummy," he chuckled, as he entered the bathroom.

Bub and Rick stared at each other until Rick looked away.

"You're really serious, huh. You really believe the dead are walking out there like in some bad horror movie."

"If you want more proof, then go down and talk to your buddy. But be careful, 'cause if you give him a chance he'll tear your throat out," Bub said.

"That's bullshit and you know it, Bub," Rick said.

"It's bullshit, huh? Well, follow me and I'll prove it," Bub said, rising from his chair and moving down the stairs know what is," Bub finished by folding his large arms in front of to the jail cells.

Greg had just exited the bathroom and was still tucking in his shirt.

"What's up, where's everyone going?" Greg asked curiously.

"Downstairs," Rick said. "Bub wants to show us proof about zombies."

"Really? Well, shit, I gotta see this," he said while moving a little faster to catch up with Rick.

Together the two men went single file down the steps to see what Bub had in mind.

Once the two men had made it to the ground floor, they stopped at the scene in front of them. Bub had taken the Sergeant out of his cell and had moved him to the desk near the stairs. The ghoul's hands had been untied and now it was only the weight of Bub's body keeping the ghoul from running around the room and trying to attack one of them.

Rick noticed the girl was awake, though she was cowering in the corner of the cell she was in. Rick didn't blame her, he had to admit he was a little scared, too.

Bub had a crazy look in his eye, reminding Rick of those evangelists on the television.

The Sergeant was bent over the desk, his head whipping around from side to side. If his mouth hadn't been covered with duct tape, Rick was pretty sure he'd be trying to take a bite out of someone, at the moment probably Bub.

Bub's left hand was holding the man down while Bub's other hand held an eight inch hunting knife, similar to a Bowie knife.

"Whoa, where'd you get that?" Rick asked, looking at the knife.

"Found it in one of the lockers upstairs. One of your cop buddies had it in his jacket. It's mine now, though," he said, smiling.

"So you want proof, right? Well, here's your goddamn proof," the large man snarled with the hunting knife raised above his head.

Bub let go of the Sergeant's back and grabbed the man's arm, then before anyone could do or say anything, Bub brought the knife down to the Sergeant's wrist and in one fluid motion pressed the blade down, severing flesh and bone.

Bub had to work at the wrist for a second, the bone giving him some trouble, but then it sliced through, the hand falling to the floor.

"Holy shit! What the hell did you that for?" Greg screamed, feeling sick.

Rick reached for his weapon. If Bub had lost it then Rick's only hope was to shoot the man quick. If Bub got within punching distance of him, then he'd be dead, as he was physically no match for the large man.

But Bub put up his hand in surrender and pointed to the Sergeant, while his other hand kept the ghoul cop from running away.

"Wait, Rick, look! Look at the guy's arm!" Bub pleaded.

Rick looked. And his mouth fell open at what he saw. The Sergeant was fine, or as fine as someone could be if they were a zombie. His head still moved from side to side, but it wasn't from pain. In fact, the wound didn't bleed that bad at all considering arteries had been severed. There was blood of course, but not what should be there if a heart had been pumping the last of its fluids.

Minutes past and the Sergeant was still the same.

"See, I told you. He's a goddamn zombie. Just like the rest of them," Bub said.

"All right fine, I guess I have to believe you, but put the guy back in his cell, will ya? I don't want him getting loose," Rick said.

Bub complied, pulling the man to the cell and tossing him inside like a bag of dirty laundry. The ghoul's head cracked against the back wall, leaving a bloody stain on the bricks, the body slumping to the floor.

Seconds later, the ghoul had recovered and was standing by the bars with its only remaining hand reaching through, trying to grab one of the survivors. It didn't take long for it to realize it had tape on its mouth and after a few failures, managed to pull it off.

Rick watched this and cringed as the duct tape was ripped from the Sergeant's face. If he'd still been alive that would have hurt like hell.

Greg walked over to his cell and gathered his things. There was no way he was going to sleep next to a zombie. Once he'd gathered everything he now owned on this earth in his hands, he went to the other end of the room and sat down on a pile of boxes.

"Okay then, let's say it's true and there are dead people running around town trying to eat us. What do we do about it?" Greg inquired.

"Well, don't look at me, I don't know," Rick said.

Greg looked to Bub. The big man just shrugged.

"I said I knew they were zombies, I didn't say I knew what we could do about it," Bub said.

"I'll tell you what we do. We gather as much food and water and weapons as we can and then we get the hell out of town. Head north to the White Mountains or something. Where there aren't a lot of people. Then we hunker down and wait for God to sort this shit out," Kim said from the back of the room.

There was a slight pause.

"Either that or we all stay here and get slaughtered like my parents and friends," she finished.

The three men looked in the corner cell to see Kim standing there.

She wore a grim determination on her face that said she was serious. Whatever the girl had experienced in the last two days was behind her now. Now all there was... was survival.

Bub was the first one to speak.

"You know, that idea isn't half bad. There are cabins and shit up there in the woods. We could stay there for quite a while; probably for the whole winter."

"But how would we get there?" Greg asked.

"The employee parking lot in back is full of cars from the other cops still on duty. I'm sure we can find some keys in one of the lockers in the changing room," Rick said.

"All right then, let's get started, it'll be light soon and the less of those bastards we have to fight, the better," Kim said, already moving up the stairs.

Rick watched her go and said to Bub: "Wow, what's got into her?"

"Don't worry about it, Rick. It's just her way of dealing with all this shit. Besides, so far she's got good ideas," Bub said, walking across the room and starting up the stairs.

Rick watched him disappear, his heavy footfalls drifting away to be replaced with his footsteps overhead as he walked around the first floor.

Greg stood up, too, and with a little smile, ran up the stairs, only seconds behind Bub.

Rick watched the Sergeant growling in his cell, the dead cop's eyes flaring red.

Rick walked over to him and stood just out of reach of his grasping hand.

Pulling his sidearm from his holster, he sighed heavily. "Sorry, Sarge, but I think if you could tell me what you'd want, I think you'd want me to do this," he said, raising the pistol even with the man's head.

Rick squeezed the trigger, sending a bullet into the Sarge's forehead. The dead man's head flew back as if punched and the rest of his body followed. The corpse lay flat on his back, its eyes staring up at the ceiling. Bits of brain, blood and cranium covered the cell floor.

Rick waited for another second to make sure the man was definitely dead. When he was sure, he opened the cell door and reached for the blanket on the cot. Then he respectively draped it over the body.

When he finished, he stepped out and closed the cell again. Better safe than sorry. Who knew what the rules of the dead were. Perhaps the Sarge would come back again.

Rick stood at the bars, grasping a metal bar in each of his raised hands.

"Rest in peace, Sarge," he said softly. Then he turned and walked up the stairs to join the others.

Behind him in the cell, the blanket began turning maroon, the material soaking up the excess blood.

Chapter 26

John awoke to the sounds of screaming filtering from outside in the night.

Jumping out of bed, he ran to the room where Lisa and the baby were sleeping.

He breathed a sigh of relief to see they were fine.

Lisa was sleeping in the room that had once belonged to the child of the house. Vincent slept quietly in the crib while Lisa was curled up on the carpeted floor next to him.

When she had finally put her baby down, it hadn't taken her too long to feel the exhaustion slip in. She had politely bid John goodnight and had gone to bed.

John had sat up a while longer, sitting in the dark living room with the shadows of the family that had once lived there surrounding him.

After a few hours had come and gone, the trials of the past few days finally hit him and he'd decided to try to get some sleep.

He'd used the bed of the husband and wife who once occupied the house, the smell of the wife's hair products still on the pillows.

While lying in the room, he couldn't help but feel unwanted. As if the ghosts of the house were telling him to leave. Despite all this, sleep did come and he'd fallen into a dreamless slumber...until now.

Another scream came to his ears and he moved down the stairs to the front door.

Looking through the small window at head height in the door, he saw a woman standing in the middle of the street; she was surrounded by a pack of dogs. She screamed again as one of them darted in and nipped at her leg.

John was about to run out and help her, already reaching for the katana, when three of the dogs attacked the woman at the same time.

One dove for her left leg, its fangs sinking deep. Another jumped high and knocked the woman to the ground, while the other dove in, its muzzle digging into her exposed throat.

With one more muffled scream the woman became silent, nothing but the sounds of the animals feeding to break the silent night.

John stood there watching, unable to take his eyes away from the grisly scene. Fifteen minutes later the animals seemed to back away from the bloody and shredded corpse.

John's jaw dropped as he watched the woman sit up and stumble to her feet. One of her legs was at an unnatural angle and the ghoul wobbled around unsure of her surroundings.

She saw the animals around her and hissed at them, the pack growling back. Then the pack backed up and ran away to be lost in the shadows of the night.

The ghoul stood still, swaying a little back and forth, then it too, wandered away to be lost in the dark.

John felt a chill run up his back. He turned away from the door and went into the kitchen. Earlier he had found a bottle of Vodka in the freezer, and while he stood alone in the kitchen, he took a swig, grimacing at the taste. He ignored it and took another shot. There was some warm cranberry juice in the fridge, so he took a few sips to clean his mouth out.

Then, with his nerves a little more stable, he went back to bed. He doubted he'd go back to sleep, but he figured he'd give it a try.

He was right.

For the rest of the night until the sun came up, he laid in bed, remembering the woman and the dogs, some images refusing to be banished.

In the next room, Lisa and her baby slept the sleep of the innocent.

* * *

The next morning he was startled out of bed by the sound of smoke detectors; the battery-operated alarms shrieked their shrill warning of fire.

John had fallen into a light sleep and now found himself unaware of his surroundings.

After a few moments, he remembered where he was and immediately ran for Lisa and the baby.

She, too, had been wakened by the smoke alarms and the two of them, plus the baby, hurried down the stairs.

While the rest of the night had passed the wind had picked up, blowing the embers of the burning houses to adjacent buildings. Like a domino effect each house had taken fire until the entire neighborhood was awash in flames, the inferno spreading faster with each house.

John moved through the house with Lisa at his side. He didn't see where the smoke was coming from.

"Stay here, I'm gonna go outside and see what's happening," he said, grabbing the katana for protection, just in case.

Throwing open the front door, he was assaulted by smoke. The house next to his was on fire, the second floor now a roaring inferno. He backed up to check on the house he was presently living in and frowned to see the roof was starting to catch fire. The dry leaves in the house's gutter starting to burn like kindling and it was just a matter of time before the whole house went up in flames like the rest in the neighborhood.

Cursing his luck, he dashed back inside, slamming the door behind him.

"All the houses in the area are on fire and so is the roof of this one. We need to go now. Gather as much food from the cabinets as you can. We don't know what the situation might be like when we leave here. Better if we stay away from populated areas. Make sure you grab as much juice and water as you can find, too."

Lisa nodded, and with Vincent fussing in her arms, she darted off to the kitchen on her assigned task.

With the katana in his hands, John ran outside with the keys to the pickup. Jumping in, he turned the vehicle around and backed it up to the front door to save time in loading the supplies.

Upon opening the pickup's door, he climbed out and walked into the woman he'd seen attacked by the dogs the night before.

Before he could do anything but stare in shock at her, she jumped him, teeth flashing in the sunlight, heading directly for his face.

He pushed his free hand under her chin and was able to turn her face away from his own before her bloody teeth touched his flesh. They both tumbled to the grass in a tangle of limbs, from a distance resembling two lovers wrestling playfully on the lawn.

The smell of decay crept into his nose and he fought his stomach to keep from throwing up. Now would not be a good time.

John had a few pounds on the ghoul and was able to roll himself on top of her. Her claw-like hands flailed at his face, trying to scratch him, the once manicured nails now broken and bloody, a few hanging on by some threads of thin gristle.

John fended her arms off and pulled the blade of the katana from its sheath.

He raised the sword and brought it down so the point pierced the ghoul's mouth.

The blade sliced through its tongue and continued through the back of her neck, where it embedded itself in the soft turf of the lawn.

The ghoul wiggled around like a fish on a hook, but couldn't pry itself loose.

John was so freaked out by what he'd just done he stood up and backed away.

The woman flailed on the ground, her hands wrapping around the blade to try and free itself.

All she got for her troubles were a few severed digits as the blade cut into her fingers from the pressure of her trying to escape.

The ghoul turned on its side, the blade cutting into its cheek. Then with a heave, pulled itself free of the blade, the sharp metal cutting through its cheek and neck as the face pulled itself away.

The ghoul rolled away, the blade wobbling in the ground, now standing straight in the dirt with red rivulets dripping down the shaft, starting from the handle.

"Oh, shit, I don't fucking believe this," John whispered as he watched the woman zombie crawl across the lawn towards him.

He ran for the katana, trying to stay out of reach of the zombies hand's, but miscalculated and fell to the ground hard as it grabbed his foot and pulled.

The soft grass cushioned his fall and he immediately reached out for the sword sticking up in the dirt, looking like the sword in the King Arthur legend.

With the ghoul pulling itself towards him with its hands on his foot, he reached out and grabbed the sword.

With a two handed grip, he sat up on his butt and swung the sword as hard as he could in a horizontal sweep. The blade sliced into the ghoul, cutting a long deep gash across her neck.

She seemed to smile, her red eyes flashing in anger; the wound barely fazing her. With his free foot, he kicked her in the face, cartilage crunching under the assault.

With a flattened nose and cut neck she looked like something out of one of his worst nightmares, but the kick in the face worked and he was able to pull himself free.

Rolling to his feet, he raised the sword over his head like a lumberjack cutting wood and brought it down with all the force he could muster.

The honed blade cut through skull and brain and only stopped when it hit her clavicle, the blade coming free after some resistance. The two pieces of the head each fell to the side, peeling back like a banana, nothing but the skin of the neck keeping them in place.

The left and right sides of the brain fell out of the skull and dropped to the lawn. The ghoul was on its knees and seemed to stay upright, its butt falling back to rest on the back heels of its shoes, perfectly balanced.

John used the tip of the katana to push the body over, feeling better when it was at least horizontal. The corpse quietly slumped to the bloody, soggy dirt and remained still, which was just fine with John.

He wiped some blood that was on his face away with his sleeve and then used a piece of the zombie's shirt to wipe the blade clean of blood. Then he went back inside.

Lisa came from the kitchen, baby Vincent still in her arms and saw the disheveled state he was in and ran over to him.

"Oh my God, what happened to you? Are you all right, are you hurt?"

He waved it all away. "I'm fine; we just had an unexpected house guest, that's all. I took care of it," he said while wiping his face with a towel as he stepped into the kitchen.

On the table were laundry buckets full of canned goods and boxes of food.

She'd been busy while he was outside.

With the smoke alarms shrieking, he yelled so she could hear him.

"All right, let's get this stuff loaded in the pickup and get the hell out of here; at least the sun's up!" He called while grabbing a box full of canned vegetables and baby food for one year olds.

She nodded. Baby Vincent had begun crying, all the noise scaring him.

Together the two of them loaded the truck's bed, making sure to toss in anything that could be of use. John threw a transistor radio in the back, maybe when they were settled they could check to see what was going on in the world. But at the moment only the here and now mattered.

Once they were packed, John ran through the house, making sure he wasn't missing anything of value. With his katana in one hand and the matching knife in his back pocket, he grabbed a few other items that may come in handy, and then he ran to the front door, where Lisa was waiting.

He stepped out first, blade in front of him, making sure it was safe for Lisa. Then he waved her out. The two climbed into the pickup, with John making sure to retrieve the sheath for the katana, after tossing the loose items from the house into the truck's tailgate.

With one last look at the house and its burning neighbors, he started the pickup and drove off into the dawn.

Behind him, the neighborhood continued to burn, the smoke covering the morning sky and tinting the clouds a dirty gray.

Chapter 27

Rick walked up the stairs from the cells quietly. The guilt of what he'd just done bothering him more than he wanted to admit.

Did he just put the Sarge down out of mercy? Or was it nothing more than the murder of a fellow officer who was obviously sick with some kind of virus or infection.

Despite what Bub had shown him with the Sarge's hand, it was still hard to come to grips with the fact that the dead were walking. After all, this was reality, not some bad Italian horror movie from the nineteen eighties that his father had been so fond of watching.

His ruminating was cut short when he reached the top of the stairs. The first floor of the police station was a flutter of activity as the companions went about the grim duty of survival.

Bub had raided the armory and was now making a pile of weapons and ammunition on one of the desks.

Kim seemed to be foraging for food. She had made a small pile of edible supplies on another desk and was even now darting into the back for more.

Rick decided to see how she was doing and followed her to the break room.

He stopped cold when he saw how she was gathering the food from the concession machines.

Glass littered the floor, the front of the machines smashed open. At the moment, Kim was digging inside the sandwich machine, gathering what was left.

"Oh, shit, did you have to smash it to pieces? I'm gonna get in so much trouble," Rick said.

Kim turned around, her hands full of sandwiches. "Trouble? Are you fucking serious? From who? Everybody's either dead or running away. Relax, you're not gonna get in trouble. There's no one left who gives a shit."

Kim strutted out of the room, her hands full of the last of the sandwiches. Rick stood very still, not quite knowing what to do.

Kim walked back into the room and stopped in front of him.

"Why don't you go get some new clothes? When we leave soon, I don't think you want to advertise you're a cop. And while you're at it see if you can find some car keys or something. If you can, try to get something with four wheel drive. We don't know what the conditions are out there and we'll probably need the traction."

Then she turned her back on him and went back to foraging.

For just a moment Rick almost wanted to say to her, "yes, sir." Everything she had just told him felt more like an order than a suggestion.

He shrugged it off, if it made the girl feel better to take charge a little, who was Rick to judge.

He moved to the back of the police station where the lockers for the policemen were and opened his own first.

In a few minutes, he was changed into the street clothes he'd worn when coming on duty Halloween night. Now that day seemed like a month ago as he looked at himself in the small mirror on his locker door.

He rubbed the five o' clock shadow that was growing on his face. With all that had happened recently, he hadn't had time to shave. He blew it off. Besides, he'd always wanted to grow a beard, anyway.

He began rummaging through some of the other lockers, looking for keys to cars or trucks.

Five minutes later, he had a little pile sitting on the bench by the lockers. Another little gem he'd found was a revolver. A Smith and Wesson .22 with a carbon steel finish sat in one of the lockers with a small box of ammunition for it. The barrel was a little over four inches and slipped perfectly into his back pocket.

Closing the locker door he decided the real owner for the weapon probably wouldn't be returning for it.

He gathered the pile of keys in his hands and walked back to the front of the station.

The others were still busy with miscellaneous tasks, so he dropped the keys on an empty desk and waited for the others to finish.

Greg saw him sitting in the corner and moved towards him.

"Hey, no more uniform, huh?" Greg stated.

Rick smiled looking down at the denim pants and sweatshirt he was now wearing.

"Yeah, I'd been in that outfit for two days and I needed a change of clothes. If you want, there's other clothes in the lockers if you want to change, too."

Greg's eyes lit up as he looked down at his dirty clothes.

"Yeah, that'd be great, thanks. With all the shit going on I hadn't even thought about it." He slapped Rick on the back and hurried to the lockers to change.

Rick saw Bub come out of the armory again and decided to go talk to him.

"Hey, Bub, do you think we'll need all that? It's not like we're going to war," Rick stated as he perused the pile of weapons and armor. "Besides we may not even have room for all this stuff."

"We'll make room if we have to, Rick. This shit is all that'll be between us and the zombies. And I don't plan on going down like that," Bub said, with a fire in his eyes.

Rick held up his hands to calm the big man down.

"All right, fine. I'm just sayin'. But do we really need bullet-proof vests and riot gear? I mean, last time I checked those people out there weren't shooting at us."

Bub stopped working for a moment and looked Rick in the eyes.

"Yeah, but there will be other people to deal with. What, you think we're the only survivors of this shit? Hell no, there'll be others and they're gonna want what we got. We have to be ready to protect ourselves. As of now, you're no longer a cop, Rick. You're just another guy trying to stay alive. The sooner you realize that the better off all of us will be," Bub told him. "Now, leave me alone, I got a lotta stuff to get." Then the big man moved off to retrieve more supplies.

Rick walked to the front door to see how it was in the street. The sun would be up in less than an hour, although the burning houses seemed to give the street the feel of a coming sunset. The fires had grown worse and off to the side of the station Rick could see there were a lot of buildings burning. If the fires continued unchecked it would just be a matter of time before the police station would be consumed as well. Already the smoke drifted across the street like a grayish fog.

Motion in the street caught his attention where a crowd of zombies (he couldn't help but call them that now) were moving about. The more Rick watched the street the more ghouls he saw.

A lot of them were sitting in bushes and in the rubble of other buildings. Rick also noticed where ever there were flames from the explosion the day before there were no ghouls. Obviously they disliked fire. He didn't blame them, but it was a kernel of knowledge to place in the back of his head.

He tried to count how many he saw, but with the shifting shadows it was hard. He figured there were at least ten in view and maybe the same in hiding.

He moved away from the doors, deciding he should see how the back was where the vehicles were parked. The sooner he knew what vehicle they'd use for their escape, then the sooner they'd know how much room there would be for supplies.

Rick walked to the back again and ran into Greg who was returning from changing his clothes. He was now wearing a pair of tan slacks and a blue sweater.

He smiled when he saw Rick. "So what do you think; is it me?"

Rick sneered back. "You look fine, look, I need someone to watch my back while I try to find us transportation out of here, and you're elected."

Rick moved off to the back fire door, making sure Greg was behind him.

"Wait! If I'm going out there, then I need a weapon, maybe some protective gear."

Rick sighed. "Fine, go see Bub. He's already got a lot of the riot gear on the desk in front. But hurry up. I'll wait here for you."

Greg nodded and with a wave disappeared down the hall.

Rick passed the time playing with the sets of keys in his hand. Most of them had alarms so it shouldn't be to hard trying to figure out what set of keys belonged to what vehicle.

As he looked through them, he immediately set a few on the windowsill in the hallway. These were the ones with keys with the logos of Honda or Toyota. He knew those vehicles were way too small to fit the four of them comfortably, plus the added room needed for supplies.

When he was done weeding out the unnecessary keys, he still had five left that were promising. He was wondering where his new friend was and was about to get the man when Greg walked back into the hall.

"How do I look?" Greg asked, standing tall in full riot gear. "I figure if one of those zombies tries to take a bite out of me, all they're gonna get is a mouthful of plastic," he said, tapping on the bulletproof chest plate.

Rick smiled, the man looked like he was about to enter a war, but he did have a point. With the riot gear on the man didn't have to worry about being bitten or clawed.

Greg strode over to him, the plastic and leather creaking in the confines of the hallway. Greg raised the nightstick and waved his hand in front of him.

"After you, my good sir. Now I've got your back."

Rick frowned and turned to the door. "All right, now be quiet, I don't know what's out here."

Rick cracked the fire door an inch and looked out into the dawn. The sun was just starting to rise, though the smoke from the fires gave it the feeling of dusk.

The area around the door was clear so Rick took another step outside.

From where he was, he was on a small landing with three stone steps that led to a cement walkway. If you followed the walkway for fifty feet you were brought to the back lot where the police station personnel parked their civilian vehicles.

The walkway was surrounded by trees on both sides, giving the feeling of walking through a tunnel.

Anything could be hiding in the shrubs or trees, just waiting for a couple of unsuspecting men to walk into their lair.

Rick took a deep breath to psych himself up and then pulled his .45. With weapon in hand, he started down the walk, with Greg creaking in his armor behind him.

Chapter 28

Tommy was having the best time of his life. Everywhere he looked he saw the seeds of his work. The town was awash in fire, the writhing flames reaching up to the morning sun as it broke its way through the clouds.

He stood in front of another two family house, ready to set it ablaze. It had become more difficult to do his work due to more and more of the crazies out on the streets.

A few times last night, he had just barely escaped from the hordes of people that seemed to be out for his blood. It was also becoming harder and harder to move around the town, as the streets became clogged with abandoned vehicles.

Many times he'd had to use his own Dodge for a ram to push other cars out of the way. Whenever possible he'd drive over lawns and sidewalks; whatever it took to get him to his next target.

He was starting to wonder if he should stop for a while, even though everything in him wanted to continue setting the town on fire. But what would happen if there were too many of the crazies to fight off? What if they trapped him?

Those thoughts still didn't deter him. Whatever was happening to the town and the world was a golden opportunity for him. He'd be damned if he was going to throw it all away because of a few nuts with cannibalistic tendencies.

The bright-red gas can pulled at his shoulder heavily, the flammable liquid sloshing around inside.

He walked up the manicured walkway, making sure to avoid the Halloween decorations scattered around the edge of the walk, the lighter for his work already in his hand.

On the porch was a child's tricycle, the handlebars decorated with tassels, while in the corner was a rake and leaf bags. Evidently before the world fell apart someone who lived in this particular house was going to do some yard chores.

Opening the cap on the gas can, he started pouring it onto the porch, making sure to do a good job. If it was one thing about Tommy, he took pride in his work.

He stepped off the porch and prepared to set his next masterpiece on fire when suddenly from the side of the house five ghouls jumped him.

The tall bushes had kept them hidden until it was too late for him to run.

Almost as if they were a team, the ghouls wrapped their hands around him and pushed him to the ground.

The gas poured out and covered him and his attackers with the flammable liquid while he struggled to get free.

A sharp pain in his leg had him looking down to see one of the ghouls chewing happily. For the moment he was fending them off, but when one grabbed his arm and started to bite into it, he knew he was lost.

Muscle and flesh were torn free as the ghoul holding his arm bit deep. Blood ran down his arm and pooled inside his shirt, feeling warm against the cool air of the morning. Another attacker dove in, and with bloody teeth, ripped a piece of his left cheek away, causing him to scream loudly in anguish.

The gas can had fallen over next to him, the liquid spilling out and collecting under him, soaking into the lawn

With his free hand, he managed to push one of his attackers away for a moment and with the lighter in his other fist, he considered his fate.

His mind weighed his options in a millisecond as the ghouls fed on his body.

One of the walking dead darted its head past his flailing arms and sunk its teeth into his throat. A half second later, his throat felt warm when blood shot out and covered his exposed flesh.

With his jugular severed, he had only seconds of consciousness left as his life's blood shot from the wound to be soaked into the already moist earth.

That's when he made his decision. Better to go out in a blaze of fiery glory, then to end up lunch to a bunch of psychos.

With his free hand he started to try and flick the lighter, but it wasn't working. Whether it was wet from blood or had a bad flint, it wasn't working.

Darkness began to descend over his vision, his fingers vainly trying to light the disposable lighter. He had enough strength for one more try, though he didn't know this. With fingers weak from blood loss, he flicked the lighter one last time.

The tiny spark erupted, a small flame burning bright in the dawn. With his last conscious thought, he smiled while the lighter slipped from his hand to land on his chest.

The small flame ignited his gas soaked clothing and the ghouls surrounding him immediately, all of them going up like a funeral pyre from Greek mythology. The flames burned his flesh and boiled what was left of his blood, but Tommy was past caring or feeling.

If he had still been alive, he would have reveled in the fact of the flames taking him into their warm embrace.

A ghoul stumbled away while its body continued to burn, its arms flailing in the air to try to put out the flames. The corpse fell onto the porch of Tommy's last target and the gas soaked porch flared into flames. The smell of burning meat filled the air, though no one was around to notice. The other ghouls stumbled away, different parts of their bodies still burning. Whether the flames on their bodies would be extinguished or not was irrelevant.

The home continued to burn, adding to the flaming town, while in the house's front yard, the blackened corpse of Tommy Garris continued to sizzle in the heat of the fire.

The head of Tommy was nothing more than a mockery of what he'd once been.

The head settled to its side and remained still, the mouth now devoid of surrounding skin. To a casual observer, it looked an awful lot like the charred face was smiling.

Even in death, he had fed the fires of his obsession.

Chapter 29

Greg and Rick crept down the cement walkway, ready for any unexpected visitors.

Rick was straining to hear any signs of movement, but every time Greg took a step, the leather of his riot suit would creak like a pair of new shoes. Rick would take two steps forward and Greg would follow with a squeak, squeak. This continued all the way to the parking lot until Rick finally turned around and glared at Greg.

Greg put his hands up in surrender. "What? It's not my fault I swear, it's the suit," he whispered.

"I don't care," Rick snapped back in a whisper. "Just try to keep it down."

The two men continued into the empty lot, the rising sun glinting off the windshields of the vehicles.

Rick looked up at the sky and frowned. Normally it would have been a beautiful sunny day, but instead the sky seemed almost overcast thanks to the pall of smoke covering the town. The temperature had dropped, as well. The Indian summer was over and had been replaced by a forty-five degree morning.

Watching all the fires that were in view, he couldn't help but wonder how the town would ever recover from the devastation it was now suffering.

Rick reached into his pocket and retrieved a few key rings. Pressing the alarm buttons on the rings, he looked for the chirping and the flash of headlights, trying to pinpoint what vehicle went with what keys.

After a few moments he had a pretty good idea what was what and headed off into the maze of cars. The squeaking of leather told him Greg was still behind him.

One of the vehicles looked very promising. A Chevy pickup with four wheel drive sat in the middle of the lot, the shiny blue, metallic paint reflecting whatever light struck its finish.

It looked to be either brand new or only a year or two old, Rick noticed, as he walked up to the front bumper. The cab was a double wide and would fit four people easily, six in a pinch. It was perfect for their needs.

The stock rims had been replaced with expensive, custom ones, the larger wheels raising the truck so high you had to reach up to climb into the cab's front seat.

Rick had the key in his hand and was ready to disable the alarm when a hand reached from underneath the truck and grabbed his leg.

One second he was standing in front of the truck, the next second the sky was staring down at him as he fell back, his head striking the concrete.

Dazed, he tried to recall what had just happened when he felt something tugging at his pants. With blurred vision he looked down and saw a zombie crawling up his body.

Greg was on the other side of the pickup, waiting for Rick to climb inside and unlock the doors and had no idea what had just happened due to the height of the vehicle.

Rick stared at the creature crawling up his body, the smell of decay overwhelming his olfactory senses.

The ghoul was one of the first, having crawled from the earth when the worms had first arrived.

Its skull was covered in decayed flesh and gobbets of meat from the feedings and battles it had been in since its awakening. Its shirt was hanging open, the autopsy stitches falling open to a hollow cavity. It had no internal organs; all had been removed before it had been laid to rest.

From behind, the ghoul looked almost laughable, the suit only complete from the front, the back cut off to make it easier for the mortician to dress the corpse before the wake and funeral.

With its bare ass sticking up in the air, the ghoul continued to crawl up Rick's body, its dried up tongue moving back and forth in its mouth as it anticipated ripping Rick's throat out. Rick had finally come back to his senses and with a shaking hand, retrieved his .45 from his hip.

Releasing the safety, he brought the gun up to the ghoul's head, and with the barrel almost touching the zombie's ear, squeezed the trigger.

Bits of rotted brains and worms shot out the side of the skull, the exit wound large enough to put a human fist through. The ghoul paused for a second until it realized it was dead for good this time and the corpse fell onto Rick, the head hitting his testicles, causing him to wince slightly.

With the sound of the gunshot, Greg ran back to Rick's side, still not aware what had happened.

"Holy shit! Why didn't you say something?" Greg yelled, reaching down and pulling the corpse off the young policeman.

"No time, whacked my head," Rick said, getting to his feet with Greg's help.

Rick was waiting for the dizziness to wear off when another zombie popped out from between two cars directly behind Greg.

With weapon still in hand, Rick brought the gun up and fired by Greg's ear, causing the man to jump away.

The ghoul behind Greg stopped moving forward as if it had run into a glass wall. Its head jerked back, a black hole appearing in its forehead. The back of its skull exploded, the grisly, pinkish spray covering the surrounding vehicles. Then it fell to the ground, taking a side mirror from the nearest car with it.

"Jesus Christ, how 'bout a little warning next time!" Greg yelled, his hand moving to his ear. There was just a hint of powder burn on his skin, but to Rick's way of thinking, it was better than being dead.

"Sorry, won't happen again," Rick quipped. "Next time I'll let the fucker eat ya."

Greg stood fuming, then pulled his hand from his ear to check for blood. Satisfied when his fingers were clean, he moved back to the passenger side of the truck and climbed into the cab.

"Shit, this is nice, you cop's do all right for yourselves. Must be all that money you guys make on those damn construction jobs you all get to 'supervise'," Greg said sitting back in the leather seats, feeling safer now that he was inside the vehicle.

Rick glanced sideways at him and then decided not to answer. Instead, he put the key in the ignition and started the engine.

The engine flared to life on the first try, a marvel of technology.

"I'm gonna park by the back door so we can load up, then we're gonna get the hell out of here," Rick said, backing out of his spot and driving around the lot.

The front tires crunched as it ran over the desiccated corpse that had attacked Rick, the worms sticking to the tires with miscellaneous gobbets of flesh and bone.

Rick moved the truck through the lot, the engine purring softly while he drove through the lines of cars. Two minutes later, he was backing the truck up to the police station, the shrubs and small trees becoming crushed under the weight of the tires.

A family of squirrels ran out, their home being disturbed. Rick saw them for only a second before their furry bodies ran up a nearby tree and were lost from sight.

When the tailgate touched the metal railing on the landing, he put the truck in park and shut off the engine.

"There, now that wasn't so hard, was it?" He smiled, climbing out of the cab. Greg frowned and followed, the two of them climbing up the stone stairs and entering the station again, Greg's suit squeaking all the way inside until the back door closed, cutting off the sound.

Outside in the trees the squirrels continued chirping, still upset that their home was destroyed and in the parking lot more walking dead appeared, drawn to the gunshots and noise of the two men.

Prey was becoming scarce as the undead fed on what was left of the population and they were still hungry, the desire to feed urging them ever onward.

Slowly, limbs stiff from rigor mortis and legs missing valuable muscle tissue moved the ghouls across the lot, following the path of the large pickup truck.

Chapter 30

"It's no use, all the damn roads are blocked," John said as he tried to maneuver around another car accident.

Since they'd left the house they had been driving around in circles. So far John had always been able to find away through the wreckage, but he was starting to wonder when they're luck would run out.

Lisa sat silently next to him; baby Vincent sleeping in her arms.

"If the roads are all blocked, then what are we going to do? The only reason we're still alive is because those things can't catch us," she spoke up, breaking her silence.

John frowned. She was right. Since they'd left the house that morning all they'd done is avoid the walking dead that were out on the streets.

If they hadn't been in the relative safety of the pickup truck, they would have been dead long ago, probably torn to pieces by the looks of some of the corpses lying scattered across the roads and sidewalks.

Thick columns of smoke from the burning buildings hung heavily over the town heavily, making visibility difficult. A few times John's hopes had gone up when he'd spotted a fire truck or a police car, but those same hopes were quickly dashed when he pulled closer to see the vehicles were abandoned, usually with blood splatter covering the shiny red or black finishes.

Groups of the undead roamed the streets and only the speed of the pickup had saved them from being overwhelmed time and again.

John reached for the katana tucked in between the seats next to him.

He had already decided if they became trapped he would kill Lisa and the baby before those bastards could get their hands on them. But for now they were safe and he hoped to keep it that way.

He found himself driving through a part of town he had never been to before.

The street would have once been considered to be a picture of suburban life. But now the homes were shattered wrecks. Windows were broken and doors hung open when the residents had rushed to evacuate.

But evacuate to where? John thought.

If a small town looked like what he was seeing then what would the big cities look like?

Lisa reached down to the radio and turned it on.

John looked at her and said: "Are you sure you want to do that? The last time you almost had a meltdown."

She sighed. "I know, but I just can't help it. Maybe it's gotten better since the last time."

She was referring to about an hour ago when she had first turned the radio on. The voice on the radio had reported that the cities were overwhelmed with the walking dead and to stay away at all costs. Police and National Guard had been overwhelmed and the streets were considered deathtraps.

Survivors were urged to hunker down and wait until the government could restore order. The voice had continued telling about other countries across the globe who had had similar outbreaks and that the authorities were helpless to stop it.

The next report told tales of hospitals and how they were nothing but morgues for the dead. But it was when the announcer's voice had cracked a little and the man had paused, the air becoming silent for a few seconds. When he came back on the air he was talking about the bible and about how we were all paying God's price for disobeying his teachings. He droned on about how the world was being punished by a plague that would ravage the earth and save the righteous; the ones who believed.

Then a commercial began to play, and three minutes later, another voice had replaced the first man. The next voice continued the reports like it was an ordinary day, the deep baritone never wavering.

John still wondered what had happened to the other announcer, had he lost it so bad they had to remove him from the station? And if so where did the man probably wind up?

With a blast of annoying static, Lisa turned the knob to the left, searching for another station, but all she received for her trouble were recorded messages of the Emergency Broadcast system.

After five minutes she gave up and turned the radio off. When she turned to look at John he noticed the bags under her eyes. He knew how she felt, he was exhausted too. The constant state of being alert was enough to drive a man mad.

His father had told him stories about what it had been like in Vietnam, about how him and his buddies were always alert for enemies, how you would never know where the next attack would come from.

As he drove through the debris strewn side roads he could only imagine what it had been like. If it was even half as bad as he felt right now, waiting for a zombie to jump at the pickup at any moment, then he figured he probably would have lost it after his first week on tour.

The smoke was heavy as the pickup drove onto the sidewalk, the houses on the next street nothing but funeral pyres of modern construction.

At the rate the fires were burning and the direction of the wind it would only be a matter of hours before the street he was now on was consumed by the conflagration.

For the tenth time that morning, he wondered how the town could be burning like it was. It just seemed unnatural that so many buildings would have caught fire so fast throughout the area.

A house on his right caught his attention. The garage door was open and when he looked around, he was pleased to see the street was empty of any threats for the moment.

Turning into the driveway, he pulled the pickup into the garage. Before Lisa could ask him what he was doing, he had hopped out of the truck and had run to the garage doors. Pulling them closed he stopped and listened for any signs of movement coming from the side door that would lead into the house.

Twenty heartbeats later he was satisfied while they may not be alone in the house at least they shouldn't have to deal with a gang of the walking dead.

He looked inside the truck's cab at Lisa and waved her to step out.

She nodded silently and with Vincent still sleeping in her arms, she exited the vehicle and walked over to John.

John put his arm around her protectively. "I think we should stay here for a while, at least until we figure out what to do. 'Cause frankly, I've just been playing it by ear so far."

"I'm not complaining, John. It's gotten us this far. I'd probably be dead by now if you hadn't saved me and Vincent would be..." She trailed off, her tears flowing freely. She tucked her head into John's shoulder and the two of them stood there for a while.

John knew how she felt. It was hard to imagine everything falling apart so fast. That in a matter of days what had taken thousands of years to create could be swept away like a janitor with a broom. Was civilization really that fragile?

After a while John gently pushed her away from him. She looked up into his eyes, her own red from crying and he smiled at her.

"Look, I don't know what sent you to me, but I'll promise you this. As long as I can, I'll take care of the both of you as if you were my own, okay?"

She smiled back, her cheeks wet with tears. "Oh, John, thank you so much," she said, hugging him hard until he was starting to fear for Vincent in between them.

"All right, all right, enough," he joked. "Now, listen, you stay here in the garage. If anything comes through that door then jump back inside the pickup, the keys are in the ignition. If I don't come back in say, half an hour, feel free to leave without me."

She was about to protest when he put his finger on her lips.

"Don't argue, remember, you have to think of Vincent."

She stopped protesting and gave in. "All right, but you be careful," she said.

"Darlin', I wouldn't have it any other way." Turning and walking to the door, he stopped and looked back to her. "Wish me luck," he said.

She blew him a kiss.

John stood still for a second, looking at this beautiful woman with a baby in her arms, wondering if despite the hell the world now found itself in, if this was his second chance to find happiness with another woman. Feeling selfish and embarrassed for even thinking such things at a time like this, he held up his hand and waved to her, then he opened the side door of the garage and stepped inside the unfamiliar home.

*   *   *

The second he stepped inside, his nose was assaulted by the smell of death and feces.

With his sword in front of him, he crept quietly into the house expecting to be attacked at any second. His heart was in his throat as he turned a corner in the house to walk into what seemed to be the living room. On the floor in front of the television was a Playstation 2,; a video game system all the kids were playing these days, though John wasn't a fan.

Walking closer, the light from outside peeking through the sides of the closed window shades, John was able to see that the Playstation and surrounding floor was covered in blood.

The smell of death was even stronger in here as he moved his way through the house.

Reaching the far end of the first floor he stopped at a painted white door. The door obviously belonged to a child, the stickers and the name tag clearly stenciled on the door. **BILLY'S ROOM** was in the middle of the door in bright colors. The smell of death was emanating even stronger from behind the door.

John paused at the door, his hand reaching for the doorknob when he heard a thumping noise coming from the other side of it.

His hand hovered by the knob, wondering if he should just walk away. After all it wasn't like he had to go in there. He could easily barricade the door and leave whatever was in there in peace.

But that wasn't his nature. He had always been a curious child and as a man he had only gotten worse. Now standing in front of the door he knew he would have to investigate, the obsession of knowing what was in there too overwhelming to resist.

Cursing his lack of self control, he turned the knob and opened the door. The door swung inward on oiled hinges, the light from the only window in the room seeping into the hall.

For a moment he thought he'd imagined the noise and the room was empty, but then without warning a small body jumped up from behind the bed and started moving towards him. The boy couldn't have been more than five years old and as John watched the child flash its bloody teeth at him, red eyes glinting in the bright room.

John's eyes took in the rest of the room and he noticed the bodies of two other people on the hardwood floor: one man and one woman. John's mind took all the available information and pieced it together in seconds. Somehow, either the mother, father or the child had become infected and had then attacked the other family members.

The mother and father rolled over on the floor and sat up. Through quick glimpses he was able to see the wounds all three of them had on their bodies, mostly on the neck, arms and face area, although the father was missing large chunks of flesh from his right leg.

With moans and groans the family started towards John. He slammed the door shut and turned the lock. A heartbeat later, the door shook in its frame, the ghouls trying to escape their prison.

John stood there holding the door shut, praying the door would hold. After a few minutes he relaxed a little, the door appeared to be holding just fine.

He stepped away from the door and stood there waiting. When he was absolutely satisfied the door would hold, he moved away to inspect the rest of the house, his ears always listening for the crash of wood of the door falling down.

The rest of the house was uneventful, the bodies only in the one room. John inspected the kitchen and found more canned goods and supplies.

Carrying as much as he could in his arms while holding the sword, he went back to the garage.

Lisa was feeding Vincent, the smell of baby poop in the air.

When he walked through the door she looked up and smiled.

"How's he doing?" John asked, placing the added supplies in the back of the pickup.

"He's good. I just changed him and I'm almost done feeding him. Is it okay in the house?"

John set his jaw and nodded no. "There's a family in one of the bedrooms. Three of them. If I don't have to, I really don't want to mess with them. They're locked in one of the rooms for now, but I don't know how long the door will hold. I figure I'll grab what I can from the kitchen and then we'll leave after a quick rest. Besides, with the fires so close, this house will just be kindling in another day or maybe less."

"Okay, but where will we go from here? You heard the radio, the cities are deathtraps."

John moved closer to her and placed his hand on the baby's head. Vincent cooed with the touch, his eyes looking up at John.

John smiled down at him. He'd never really thought of himself the fatherly type and then bang, here he was with the little guy in front of him relying on John to keep him safe.

John looked at Lisa. "I figure we should head north into New Hampshire, maybe go deep into the woods where there aren't a lot of people. Then we wait, other than that, I got nothin'," he said, removing his hand from Vincent's head.

Lisa was quiet, her attention focused on her baby. Then she looked up, her eyes filled with hope.

"All right, that sounds good, when do we leave?"

"An hour or so, let's take this time to relax, I know I'm exhausted. Then we'll go. I should be able to make my way to 95 by the back roads. Then we just have to hope the highway's clear."

Lisa nodded and walked away to sit on some boxes in the corner of the garage, her attention again focused on her baby.

John went to the driver's seat of the pickup and sat down. Closing his eyes, he soon drifted off into a light sleep. In his daydream the world was fine and the worst thing he had to worry about was an upcoming health physical.

While the three survivors rested, the town continued to burn and the walking dead continued to feed, the world collapsing from the inside out.

Chapter 31

Rick and Greg strode into the main room of the police station with large smiles on their faces.

"We have transportation," Rick called to the others.

Bub looked up from the pile of weapons he had accrued on the desk.

"That's great, man, what did ya get us?" The large man asked.

"It's a big Chevy truck with room for all of us. Wait till you see the size of the tires," Greg said. "If any of those zombies get in our way, we can just drive over them." He smiled while placing his nightstick on a nearby desk.

"So, when do we leave?" Rick asked the others.

Kim spoke up first. "We've almost gathered everything worth taking, so once we're done we should probably go. The sooner the better, too. That way we've got the whole day to travel before dark."

"I wonder how hard it's gonna be to get up north? You think other people thought the same thing as us?" Bub asked Kim.

She shrugged slightly. "Sure, it's possible, but that's why we're leaving soon, hopefully before the highway gets too bad." Kim walked away to search out more supplies.

Rick watched her go. She hadn't cried or yelled since she'd come around after they'd saved her from her car and Rick couldn't help wondering how she was really doing inside. Some people kept their emotions bottled up so tightly that when it finally became too much for them, they would literally explode, usually losing it at the worse possible time in the process.

Rick didn't want that to happen when he and the others might need her sharp and focused. He decided right here and now that he'd keep an eye on her in case she started to slip.

He noticed Bub looking at him and he walked over to the man.

"Check out all this shit, we're ready to fight a goddamn war," he said, motioning to all the weaponry and ammunition.

There were pistols, revolvers, shotguns and tasers and a few bottles of tear gas. Rick couldn't help but wonder how effective the last items would be on walking dead people, but at least the smoke would be good cover.

"That's great, Bub. Looks like you stripped the place clean."

"Fuckin A, if it wasn't nailed down I took it. Besides, it's not like any-one else is gonna use it."

Rick thought about that for a moment. If the National Guard or the State Police were going to come and help they should have been here by now. So Bub was probably right.

"Okay, sounds fine with me. I've got to use the bathroom. I'll be right back."

"All right, but don't forget, if you shake it more than twice that means you're playin' with it."

Rick smiled half-heartedly at Bub's crude and outdated joke and then headed off for the bathroom.

Soon they would be ready to go and with the hordes of the undead piling up outside it would be a challenge to load the truck and escape.

But he had confidence in the men and one woman he now found himself with.

One way or another they would survive.

*　*　*

An hour later the four of them gathered in the main room of the station to discuss an exit strategy.

Rick had just checked the back door and was unhappy to find more than thirty ghouls wandering around. The walking corpses knew they were inside the building and they wanted in.

The front of the station was no better. The fires had forced the undead to evacuate large portions of the town, sending them to the immediate area surrounding the police station.

While there were thirty or so ghouls in back, there had to be almost double in front. For the moment, the undead horde was docile, just wandering around while others had simply sat down. But when anything living came near them, they would burst into activity and attack. Which was the case when a stray dog had wandered through the street, not comprehending the danger it was in.

The ghouls had surged toward the animal, completely surrounding it and with teeth and hands had ripped it to pieces.

Now all that was left of the animal was a maroon spot on the left side of the street and a few tufts of hair. Flies sat in the small, drying puddle attempting to gain what nourishment they could.

Rick turned away from the door and returned to Bub's side.

"Jesus, there's a lot of them out there. It's gonna be a bitch trying to load up all the supplies before we can go," Rick said.

"Don't you worry about that. I've already got a plan," Bub said, a smile creasing his unshaven face.

"Oh, yeah? What, fill me in."

Bub placed his hand on Rick's shoulder. "Later, buddy, later. Right now I've got to use the head. I'll be right back," Bub said, moving to the bathroom door.

Rick stood at the weapon's table fingering a strap to a double-barrel shotgun, when Kim came over to him and looked up at his face. Her expression was one of contempt, like a Captain criticizing one of his men.

"Just what do you think you're doing?" She asked.

"What do you mean, I'm not doing anything?" Rick said defensively.

"Exactly, there's a lot of work to be done before we can leave and you're standing around shooting the shit."

"Hey, wait a minute. I did just get the truck, didn't I?" He replied.

"Yeah, and you did a great job, now, how 'bout carrying some of the food into the hall by the back door. We're gonna have to move fast when we start loading it."

Rick nodded in agreement. "Okay, you're right, I'm going," he said, going to the food supplies and taking a handful. While he started making trips back and forth to the back door, he thought about his predicament.

He was trapped inside his own police station with a guy who was once a prisoner, a teenage girl with a Patton complex, and an office supply worker. Outside in the streets, the town was burning to the ground and the walking dead were everywhere, just waiting to take a bite out of his ass.

Dropping an armful of supplies and going back for more, he at least took heart in the fact it couldn't get any worse.

At least he prayed it wouldn't.

Chapter 32

Half an hour later, the four survivors were ready to go. The hallway was wall to wall supplies. Guns and ammo, on top of the food supplies were now mixed in with blankets, flashlights, and sheets. Anything that could be salvaged from the station was now in the hallway.

The four survivors stood one in front of the other in a single line. Greg was still in his riot gear and he and the other three were wearing gas masks.

Bub's plan was simple. Two of them would step outside with weapons drawn and cover the other two while they loaded the supplies. Bub would throw the tear gas canisters around the pickup to help keep them hidden. He already figured the actual tear gas would have no effect on their already dead attackers but at least the smoke would keep them disoriented…hopefully.

"All right, ready? I'm gonna start tossing canisters out. Then me and Rick will keep the two of you covered. But move quickly, cause once we're out of ammo, I don't think there'll be time to reload," Bub said.

On top of the 12-gauge shotgun in his hands he had a large service pistol strapped to his hip. Rick was pretty sure it was the S&W .38, Model 640, he'd seen on the table earlier.

Rick had his .45 in his hand and the .22 he'd found tucked into the front of his pants for quick access. With a nod from Bub, the large man opened the door a crack and peeked outside.

It was hard for the man to see clearly with his face wearing the gas mask, but he was able to discern the area around the pickup had zombie problems.

Absently he admired the truck Rick had found, the finish glinting in the sun. The smoke was already thick outside from the countless fires surrounding the police station and Bub was glad he was wearing the mask. Even if he wasn't about to toss canisters of tear gas around the back landing.

He closed the door and turned to the three masked faces.

"There's a bunch of them out there and once we start shooting, we'll probably get more, so let's do this quick and get the hell out of here."

Bub turned and with a canister in hand opened the door wide. Even with the smoke, it was still brighter outside than in the building, and Bub's eyes dilated from the glare of the day.

He pulled the pin and threw the canister, not exactly seeing where it was going, while his eyes adjusted to the light difference. But it didn't matter. The canister flew ten feet to land in the bushes, the smoke already billowing from it. Bub followed the first with three more, using everything the armory had stocked. He figured what the hell would they need tear gas for in a world full of zombies, anyway?

Once all the hissing canisters were scattered around the area surrounding the pickup, he stepped out onto the faded concrete platform.

Jumping over the metal railing, he landed in the bed of the truck. He was quickly followed by Greg. Rick stayed on the landing while Kim started to run supplies back and forth to the truck where Greg would catch them and drop them into the truck's bed.

The moment Bub's feet hit the metal tailgate, the zombie's began to attack. Fresh meat was in front of them and they were hungry.

From up in the truck's bed Bub had the advantage of height and when the first ghoul stumbled into view, he leveled the shotgun down at its head and sent a barrage of death directly at its face.

With a spray of blood and brains, the face disappeared and the body fell away, only to be replaced by two more. Using the stock of the weapon, Bub cracked another one over the head, the skull splitting. It fell to the trampled grass with gray matter leaking out of its fractured cranium. Its brethren barely noticed their fallen brother, their eyes only on the meat in front of them.

While Kim and Greg continued to load the supplies, Rick took shots from the cement landing. With the railing surrounding him, all he had to worry about was the steps, which were open.

The first ghoul in line, a woman in a housecoat, Rick noticed in the chaos, started up the stairs only to fall back away when a small hole appeared in her forehead.

The woman fell back onto the others behind her, slowing the others down for a fraction of a second. Then the body was on the ground and the other undead walked over it. Rick kept firing, not keeping track of how many rounds he was using, when his weapon clicked on an empty cylinder.

Cursing to himself, he reached for the .22 just as a face darted at him. He jammed the barrel of the gun into its mouth and squeezed the trigger with the barrel pointed at an upward angle. The head bucked back as the small caliber bullet bounced around inside its skull, pulping its brain to mush.

It fell in front of him on the landing, adding to the others he'd shot. There was a pretty formidable barricade of bodies on the steps now as each one Rick had shot had fallen on top of the previous one. Now the zombies had to try to crawl over its predecessors, only to be met with a bullet in the head from Rick.

For ten minutes Bub and Rick shot and killed ghoul after ghoul until Rick wondered if it would ever end or if it would continue until he finally ran out of bullets and was overwhelmed.

Bub shot another with the shotgun, the torso was torn apart from the fusillade of bullets as the barrage riddled the body. It fell away to be replaced by others.

Then Kim's voice cut through the noise of gunshots and moaning.

"That's it we're done! Let's get the hell out of here!"

Bub yelled to the others. "You heard the little lady, it's time to go. Rick, get the keys and start the truck!"

Keys! Oh shit, he didn't have the keys, he realized as he felt around his body with his free hand, pausing for a moment to shoot another corpse down. The bullet entered its left eye and continued into the brain, dropping the ghoul to the earth with the others.

He was about to yell to Bub, that he didn't have them, when Greg jumped off the tailgate with the keys in his hand. "I got them!" Greg yelled to the area.

Rick sighed with relief; he had forgotten he'd given them to Greg before they had filled the hallway with supplies. They had all agreed that with Greg's riot suit he was the best choice to have to fight his way to the driver's seat.

Greg hit the ground running, his nightstick in his hand. Swinging it like a club, he knocked ghouls aside like ten pins. They tried to bite him and claw him, but the leather and plastic of his suit did its job well and he made it to the driver's door in one piece. Through the noise of the gunshots, Rick heard the distinctive beep of the alarm disarming.

Then Greg opened the door and climbed inside. A ghoul tried to climb inside with him and Bub leaned over the front of the truck and shot the walking corpse in the back. While it didn't mind the shot, the impact gave it pause and Greg kicked it away and slammed the door shut, blood covering the inside door panel.

A second later, the engine roared to life and the truck bucked slightly as Greg put the transmission into drive.

Rick glanced at Kim, who was still on the landing, hiding behind him. The tough girl from earlier was gone as she witnessed the brutality surrounding her.

Bub called to them both. "Just jump in the bed with me, once we're clear from here we can get inside!" He yelled while blowing another ghoul's head off. Only half the blast caught the head and the other half with its one eye looked around for a few moments until Bub whacked it in the head with the stock of his shotgun.

The face fell away to be lost under the trampling feet of its brethren.

For a moment Bub was clear, the ghouls not able to climb the side of the truck, the custom tires giving the vehicle extra height. He held out his hand for Kim to take and with a gentle shove from Rick, she jumped the railing to land in a pile of blankets.

"Come on, Rick, let's go!" Bub yelled, while Greg revved the engine for emphasis.

Rick shot one more zombie, the .22 bullet striking it in the shoulder. The ghoul shrugged it off and continued climbing over its brethren to get to Rick.

Rick ignored it and climbed over the railing. Just as he jumped, the zombie was able to grab his flailing leg. Rick felt himself stop in midair and then gravity took over and he dropped like a lead weight, his head striking the metal of the tailgate.

He was dazed from the impact and as his vision cleared he saw four ghouls standing in front of him, ready to pounce and tear him to shreds.

He screamed in panic and fear and closed his eyes. Then he felt the world moving under him and opened his eyes to see the ghouls receding into the smoke of the tear gas.

Greg had picked the perfect time to hit the gas. Bub reached down and grabbed his collar and pulled him closer to the rear window of the truck.

There was still a threat of falling off the bed as it bounced over bodies, the truck bouncing around like it was four wheeling.

Five minutes later, they were clear of the area and everyone took off their gas masks

The air tasted of wood and other things best not thought of, but was still a hundred times sweeter than wearing the gas masks.

Rick lay in the bed, staring up at the smoky sky.

"Wow, that was close," he breathed.

"Tell me about it," Bub said from his side. "I saw you fall and thought it was over for you."

"Yeah, so where to now?" Rick inquired over the noise of the truck.

"Greg says he knows the back roads to the highway, we should be there in about twenty minutes or so if the roads are manageable," Bub said.

Rick just nodded. He looked at Kim sitting on the other side of him. She had a faraway look as she watched what was left of her hometown burn.

Rick placed a hand on hers and she turned to look at him. Her eyes were wet from crying. Rick squeezed her hand and she gave him a brief smile. More for show than a true sentiment, Rick thought.

*   *   *

The pickup truck continued through the town, flames shooting up to the sky like orange and red tentacles, from the houses lining the street.

Rick wondered if this is what hell would be like, with flames everywhere while demons try to eat you.

Greg was able to maneuver around the wreckages. What he couldn't go around, he sometimes went through. The large pickup up to the task.

Turning sharply at the next corner, Greg stepped on the gas pedal, knowing the onramp to I-95 was just around the corner, when another smaller pickup shot out of another side street and was now directly in his path.

Greg tried to swerve and hit the brakes, but even as he tried, he knew he wouldn't be able to stop in time.

The large Chevy hit the smaller pickup on the driver's side, pushing in the door and causing the Chevy to stop hard in the road.

The startled passengers in the bed were thrown against the rear window, and Rick was almost thrown to the road, before Bub grabbed his jacket and held on.

With the sound of breaking glass and crunching metal the two vehicles became one.

For a moment everything went still, nothing but a sparrow in a nearby tree chirping its song.

Then slowly, everyone came around. Only a few minutes had past since the two vehicles had struck each other and Greg was the first one to react.

He jumped from the truck, his riot suit protecting him from the impact, and ran to the other vehicle.

Moving to the passenger side, he saw a woman sitting there. She was moving and with a few heaves Greg was able to open her stuck door. She would have fallen to the cement if Greg hadn't caught her and helped her out of the pickup.

That was when he saw the baby in her arms.

Muttering a silent prayer to God, he pulled back the blanket the baby was swaddled in. Big blue eyes looked up at him and a tiny mouth smiled.

Greg sank to the street next to the woman; thanking God the baby was fine.

The woman became more focused, the trauma of the crash wearing off. Her face went into panic mode and she looked around.

Greg placed his hand on her shoulder and tried to calm her.

"It's all right, you were in an accident, but your baby's okay," he said.

The woman sat up and looked at the pickup. Then she yelled to the driver.

"John? John! Oh my God, is he all right? Please someone check on him," she pleaded from the street. The baby started to fuss and she held him close.

"I'm on it," Bub said, moving to the front of the Chevy.

The accident looked worse than it was, the smaller pickup taking the brunt of the impact.

Bub went around the other side while Rick and Kim went to the woman.

The big man reached inside and felt the driver's pulse. For a second there didn't seem to be one, until Bub moved his fingers to the correct place and then felt the steady rhythm of the man's heart.

Bub stood up and called to the others "For what it's worth, he's got a pulse. Other than that..." Bub shrugged his big shoulders.

Rick looked around the road they were on. It was a back road with only a few houses in sight. For the moment the road was empty. He looked behind him to see the smoke rising into the sky, the trees blocking anything else from view.

He turned to see Bub reaching into the small pickup through the passenger's side to retrieve the man. Rick quickly moved to help, although he doubted the big man needed it.

Together they were able to set the man onto the street. Rick gave the man a cursory inspection and except for a nasty gash on the man's forehead, he appeared to be intact; although internal bleeding might be a problem later.

By now the woman was up and with Greg's help made it to the side of the hurt man.

"John? Don't you die on me. Not after everything we've been through," she said, tears welling up in her eyes to fall onto John's shirt.

John groaned and raised his hand to his forehead, immediately pulling it away when the wound shot pain into his head from being disturbed.

"Ohhh, what happened?" He whispered.

"I'm afraid I did," Greg said, kneeling down next to the prone man.

"Who would think I had to worry about hitting another car out here? Shit, I thought I was the only one on the road."

John rolled onto his side and vomited up some of his lunch. Rick was pleased to see there was no blood mixed in with the vomit.

"Can someone help me up, please?" John asked.

Bub leaned in and with one fluid motion the man found himself standing up.

"There ya go, buddy. Whoa, easy does it," Bub said, catching the man from falling over. Apparently John was still dizzy.

Five minutes went by with John catching his breath and the others making cooing noises at the baby. They found out the woman's name was Lisa and the baby was Vincent.

While the others talked, John, Rick and Bub walked over to the vehicles.

"Oh, shit, would you look at that. My truck's ruined," he said, kicking the yellow globe that had been knocked from the roof of his pickup from the accident. "What the hell are me and Lisa going to do now?" John said; the worry in his voice apparent.

Rick and Bub looked at each other and Bub nodded.

"You could come with us," Rick said. "We've got plenty of room and supplies."

Bub noticed the supplies John had in the back of his own truck's bed and smiled.

"Hell, yeah, you can add your stuff to ours and join us. We're going up north to the mountains, probably. Figure we'll wait out this shit storm and come back later."

John smiled, but then winced when his cut hurt. "No kidding, that's what me and Lisa were doing. At least until we got creamed."

Bub called to Greg who ran over to the other men. "Hey, Greg, why don't you back up and separate the trucks. If we need to go in a hurry, I don't want to have to worry about it."

Greg nodded. "Sure, no prob'." The man ran to the Chevy and climbed in. A moment later the engine roared to life and with the sound of tearing metal, backed away from the smaller vehicle.

John winced while he watched. He was damn lucky. If the kid had been going a little faster he might not have survived the impact.

The truck sat idling in the street, the front bumper was a little warped, that being the only sign that the large pickup had been in an accident.

Rick looked up the street where the few scattered house were and frowned. There were people walking towards them and by the way they shambled, he doubted very much they were healthy.

"Bub, we've got company," Rick called.

"Shit. Look, let's save the introductions for later. For now I think we should keep moving," Bub suggested.

John nodded and went to see to Lisa and the baby.

"Hello, people! There are dead people coming to eat us!" Rick said, pointing down the road, behind them.

The others all looked to where he was pointing and quickly got to work. With all hands to help, it took less than five minutes to transfer the supplies from the bed of the smaller wrecked vehicle to the larger one. When they were finished, the approaching ghouls were only a few feet away.

Rick raised his .45, now with a fresh clip, and prepared to fire when Bub placed his hand on his arm.

"Don't bother, we're done here. Leave them alone. Besides, you might need that ammo later."

Rick looked at Bub and lowered his weapon, the advice sound.

Every time he saw a zombie, he now wanted to kill it. But the better move would be to ignore the ghoul if he wasn't being threatened by it.

Just leave the walking corpse be.

Sound words for any man in history against any foe.

Everyone piled into the inside of the truck except for Rick and Bub, who hopped into the bed. Then Greg drove off down the road, the onramp only seconds away.

Rick looked through the rear window into the cab where Lisa and John sat with the others.

"You know what, Bub? That new guy looks awfully familiar to me. I just can't place where I've seen him before."

Bub shrugged. "Not like it really matters, does it?"

Rick shook his head. "No, I suppose not, but still..." He trailed off, realizing it didn't really matter. He'd probably seen the guy at the Halloween block party or at a local convenience store, that's all. He leaned back onto the pile of supplies and tried to get more comfortable. They had a long ride in front of them.

The large tires of the pickup were formidable, and even if the highways were choked with cars, the large truck could easily drive on the lush green grass that separated the north and south sides of the highway from each other.

With the sun high in the sky, the smoky air soon thinned as the pickup drove north on the empty highway, away from the flaming town of Wakefield.

None of the survivors knew what to expect once they crossed the New Hampshire border, but they had food, weapons, ammunition and most of all, each other.

The rest would work itself out on its own.

DEADFREEZE
By Anthony Giangregorio

THIS IS WHAT HELL WOULD BE LIKE IF IT FROZE OVER.

When an experimental serum for hypothermia goes horribly wrong, a small research station in the middle of Antarctica becomes overrun with an army of the frozen dead.

Now a small group of survivors must battle the arctic weather and a horde of frozen zombies as they make their way across the frozen plains of Antarctica to a neighboring research station.

What they don't realize is that they are being hunted by an entity whose sole reason for existing is vengeance; and it will find them wherever they run.

THE MONSTER UNDER THE BED
By Anthony Giangregorio

Rupert was just one of many monsters that inhabit the human world, scaring children before bed. Only Rupert wanted to play with the children he was forced to scare.

When Rupert meets Timmy, an instant friendship is born. Running away from his abusive step-father, Timmy leaves home, embarking on a journey that leads him to New York City.

On his way, Timmy will realize that the true monsters are other adults who are just waiting to take advantage of a small boy, all alone in the big city.

Can Rupert save him?

Or will Timmy just become another statistic.

DARK PLACES
By Anthony Giangregorio

A cave-in inside the Boston subway unleashes something that should have stayed buried forever.

Three boys sneak out to a haunted junkyard after dark and find more than they gambled on.

In a world where everyone over twelve has died from a mysterious illness, one young boy tries to carry on.

A mysterious man in black tries his hand at a game of chance at a local carnival, to interesting results.

God, Allah, and Buddha play a friendly game of poker with the fate of the Earth resting in the balance.

Ever have one of those days where everything that can go wrong, does? Well, so did Byron, and no one should have a day like this!

Thad had an imaginary friend named Charlie when he was a child. Charlie would make him do bad things. Now Thad is all grown up and guess who's coming for a visit?

These and other short stories, all filled with frozen moments of dread and wonder, will keep you captivated long into the night.

Just be sure to watch out when you turn off the light!

DEAD TALES: SHORT STORIES TO DIE FOR
By Anthony Giangregorio

In a world much like our own, terrorists unleash a deadly disease that turns people into flesh-eating ghouls.

A camping trip goes horribly wrong when forces of evil seek to dominate mankind.

After losing his life, a man returns reincarnated again and again; his soul inhabiting the bodies of animals.

In the Colorado Mountains, a woman runs for her life, stalked by a sadistic killer.

In a world where the Patriot Act has come to fruition, a man struggles to survive, despite eroding liberties.

Not able to accept his wife's death, a widower will cross into the dream realm to find her again, despite the dark forces that hold her in thrall.

These and other short stories will captivate and thrill you. These are short stories to die for.

SOULEATER
By Anthony Giangregorio

Twenty years ago, Jason Lawson witnessed the brutal death of his father by something only seen in nightmares, something so horrible he'd blocked it from his mind.

Now twenty years later the creature is back, this time for his son. Jason won't let that happen.

He'll travel to the demon's world, struggling every second to rescue his son from its clutches.

But what he doesn't know is that the portal will only be open for a finite time and if he doesn't return with his son before it closes, then he'll be trapped in the demon's dimension forever.

ROAD KILL: A ZOMBIE TALE
By Anthony Giangregorio

ORDER UP!

In the summer of 2008, a rogue comet entered earth's orbit for 72 hours. During this time, a strange amber glow suffused the sky.

But something else happened; something in the comet's tail had an adverse affect on dead tissue and the result was the reanimation of every dead animal carcass on the planet.

A handful of survivors hole up in a diner in the backwoods of New Hampshire while the undead creatures of the night hunt for human prey.

There's a new blue plate special at DJ's Diner and Truck Stop, and it's you!

THE DARK
By Anthony Giangregorio

DARKNESS FALLS

The darkness came without warning.

First New York, then the rest of United States, and then the world became enveloped in a perpetual night without end.

With no sunlight, eventually the planet will wither and die, bringing on a new Ice Age. But that isn't problem for the human race, for humanity will be dead long before that happens.

There is something in the dark, creatures only seen in nightmares, and they are on the prowl.

Evolution has changed and man is no longer the dominant species.
When we are children, we are told not to fear the dark, that what we believe to exist in the shadows is false.

Unfortunately, that is no longer true.

DEAD RECKONING: DAWNING OF THE DEAD

By Anthony Giangregorio

THE DEAD HAVE RISEN!

In the dead city of Pittsburgh, two small enclaves struggle to survive, eking out an existence of hand to mouth.

But instead of working together, both groups battle for the last remaining fuel and supplies of a city filled with the living dead.

Six months after the initial outbreak, a lone helicopter arrives bearing two more survivors and a newborn baby. One enclave welcomes them, while the other schemes to steal their helicopter and escape the decaying city.

With no police, fire, or social services existing, the two will battle for dominance in the steel city of the walking dead.

But when the dust settles, the question is: will the remaining humans be the winners, or the losers?

When the dead walk, the line between Heaven and Hell is so twisted and bent there is no line at all.

RISE OF THE DEAD
By Anthony Giangregorio

DEATH IS ONLY THE BEGINNING

In less than forty-eight hours, more than half the globe was infected.

In another forty-eight, the rest would be enveloped.

The reason?

A science experiment gone horribly wrong which enabled the dead to walk, their flesh rotting on their bones even as they seek human prey.

Jeremy was an ordinary nineteen year old slacker. He partied too much and had done poorly in high school. After a night of drinking and drugs, he awoke to find the world a very different place from the one he'd left the night before.

The dead were walking and feeding on the living, and as Jeremy stepped out into a world gone mad, the dead spotting him alone and unarmed in the middle of the street, he had to wonder if he would live long enough to see his twentieth birthday.

LIVING DEAD PRESS

Where the Dead Walk

www.livingdeadpress.com

DEAD UNION
By Anthony Giangregorio

BRAVE NEW WORLD

More than a year has passed since the world died not with a bang, but with a moan.

Where sprawling cities once stood, now only the dead inhabit the hollow walls of a shattered civilization; a mockery of lives once led.

But there are still survivors in this barren world, all slowly struggling to take back what was stripped from their birthright; the promise of a world free of the undead.

Fortified towns have shunned the outside world, becoming massive fortresses in their own right. These refugees of a world torn asunder are once again trying to carve out a new piece of the earth, or hold onto what little they already possess.

HOSTAGES

Henry Watson and his warrior survivalists are conscripted by a mad colonel, one of the last military leaders still functioning in the decimated United States. The colonel has settled in Fort Knox, and from there plans to rule the world with his slave army of lost souls and the last remaining soldiers of a defunct army.

But first he must take back America and mold it in his own image; and he will crush all who oppose him, including the new recruits of Henry and crew.

The battle lines are drawn with the fate of America at stake, and this time, the outcome may be unsure.

In a world where the dead walk, even the grave isn't safe.

www.ingramcontent.com/pod-product-compliance
Lightning Source LLC
Chambersburg PA
CBHW070639170726
48291CB00003B/1067